Thanks!

the Knight Fighter

by

alexander cousins

an Art Stream Media Limited Publication

Follow Raymond Knight @ facebook.com

or email artstreammedia@mail.com

for Trailers, News about the sequels and Free Book offers

This is a work of fiction. Names, characters, business, events and incidents are the products of the author's imagination. Any resemblance to actual persons, living or dead, or actual events is purely coincidental.

ISBN 978-1-7395464-0-3

contact the author or publisher via email:
artstreammedia@mail.com

Funding For Tracy . . .

Every copy of the Knight Fighter sold goes 100% toward Charity. Please know that for every copy you buy, you will be helping a devoted mother gift her young son precious more time to spend together

Diagnosed with a rare form of Brain tumor, Tracy Verblis is currently undergoing a pilot treatment scheme, and her commitment and sacrifice to this cause could greatly aid and encourage future patients

Please visit their GoFundMe site to learn more :- https://gofund.me/2e4aa281

Part One

1

There was a sense that things could not go on as before. Nightly news broadcasts only ever lurched from one crisis to the next, elected officials had very little encouraging to say, pollution seemed to be making the air harder to breathe and it was turning the river that ran through the city into some kind of toxic stew. People put their heads down and worked all the more harder, as if they sensed a clock was ticking down. Despite all the advances in convenience, the flashy gadgets and expensive distractions, life was tough, and getting tougher. Expectations were set low, but they were consistently not met even then.

The city of Templeton was apparently the third largest in the North West, but no one seemed to care or benefit from this fact. Once a modest and thriving seaside settlement, the apartment blocks and high rises had reproduced until Templeton's vast spread now staggered under the pressure to sustain and house its population. It ground on, despite a decline in law and order and investment, continuing to grow and expand in size, stubbornly. The criminal underworld expanded also, to match the opportunity, and the city matured into a rough and unforgiving place, like most any other; useful if you could find a way to make it work, but merciless if you could not keep up.

For most of those that lived in Templeton, they remained there because it was all they had ever known, or they simply did not have the means to leave. More often than not, the weather seemed set on exaggerating the hopelessness, and just like the evening before, a light rain fell over the blinking, swarming expanse, as if to slow and deter the endless passage of busy lives, churning around the city's pot-holed streets.

He felt some comfort from the thrum of the crowds, the thousands walking the streets with him then, pushing and dodging and rushing to where they needed to be, to do what they needed to do. He kept his face composed and his strides purposeful. It was easy to conceal his deadly need from them, to act as if he too were just like one of them. As if he had somewhere he needed to be, and he had something he needed to do. Something ordinary, normal, and not the brutal act of savagery he had in mind.

***Kill him. Stop his heart, switch him off, shut him down. Eradicate him from existence*.**

If he had ever asked himself if he could kill, he would have said no, not ever. How could anyone deliberately turn their back on the civilized world and commit the ultimate sin, cross the line from human to monster and reject the principles that most hold godly, and decent? Never him; he could never take another's life in vengeance, in defence, or in duty. It took a special mindset to take someone's life with cold-blooded intention; a unique determination.

That was until about eight years ago. It was only then, at that late stage in his life, that his thinking had been changed, and he had cultivated a different creature from the man he once identified as himself.

Up until that time, he had made the conscious effort to be one of life's good guys; a decent man, straight-talking, level-headed, dependable, even humble. He had thought it was the right thing to do. But then the world he thought he knew turned upside down, revealed a side so dark and horrifying that it seemed to him to mock his former way of thinking. Life as he had known it was simply erased, and a pain had matured in his soul and corrupted his entire being, skewing his manner, his personality and all that he had held sacred. He chose not to resist the slowly advancing change, and he had allowed the dark to fester inside of him.

No spite, no mercy, no judgement. Just do it. End it. End him. Make him dead. Kill him.

The change was a cancerous progress, a mutation that took root and, over the last three years, had established control of his actions, of his thoughts. He submitted to the change, and like shedding an old skin and growing into a new one, he had learned to forget his old self and welcome the new being that replaced it; Felt its desires, sensed its impulses and flexed its muscles; Breathed him in, and adapted to the rhythm of a new pulse and new heart beat.

He pushed his new body to the extremes of training that he knew were necessary, and ate only to fuel this compulsion. He hurt and bled and sweat, and gradually grew stronger, until the day came when he decided he was ready; That his new self was strong enough to be introduced to the outside world; an ancient force, reborn into reality. Tonight he would cross the line, from man to monster.

Kill him. Make him dead.

Not long now. This city, that until recently was refuge to his enemies, to hide within and infest at the edges like an infection, this now was his hunting ground. The particular object of his hunt tonight was just one of these parasites. A worthless wretch, of whom the dark of the world had corrupted into something perverse and toxic. This creature infected those around him with the poison that he sold them, profiting off the weakness of their kind. He knew this because he had watched him, had observed him over many months, and learned the habits of his prey as well as he knew his own. This world would be well rid of this parasite, and he was the one to rid it of him.

He stopped walking. There were only two or three other people standing around at the bus stop, and here he waited, with the patience and controlled breathing he had perfected over the years. After a short interval he glanced up, and scanned the other side of the street.

Opposite the stop, an underground train station released commuters onto escalators rising up to the pavement. He studied every face that emerged, until his vision locked onto the one he knew so well. Here he was, the one he hunted. As if sensing the anticipation he radiated, the target's head turned, met his gaze, and gave a discreet nod of acknowledgement. Then the target began to walk away, the sign as agreed. The invitation to follow.

Kill.

The one he now followed moved quickly through the crowds. Given the slight build, his prey was able to weave and slide between the people with ease, but he kept him dead centre in his cross hairs. This was one that was adept at evading detection and suspicion, thrived off it. But not for much longer.

A twist, and his quarry left the main high street to

disappear within a chasm opened up in the face of one of the great buildings beside them. He followed, into a narrow alley, dark, and private. It would be just the two of them, him and his prey, alone. The alley expanded into a small courtyard, and here the object of his pursuit had taken position beneath the metal railing of a low balcony. The target's foot tapped impulsively as the one now nodded his head and spoke from between stained teeth.

"You got the cash? Let me see it."

He locked eyes with his prey and held his stare, in silence, for slightly longer than he felt was comfortable. It had the desired effect. The little man shifted impatiently from one foot to the other.

"Don't fuck me around, you got it or not? I got people who would kill for this shit."

He braced his body into complete stillness, steadying his breathing against the anticipation, and then he raised one hand in front of him.

"Let me see the stuff first."

"Aw, what is this now? You're not shopping for fucking truffles!"

The silence returned. With another curse, the dealer reached into his inside jacket pocket and handed over the small, tightly wrapped parcel.

He accepted the parcel, made a show of weighing it in his hand, and then turned his back on the man, who protested again in exasperation. Calmly, he pocketed the parcel and shucked off his jacket, letting it fall to the ground and revealing the full glory of what he wore beneath. Then, he turned around to face the man again. For a pleasing moment, he watched the target's eyes widen in surprise, regarding him silently, giving his appearance time to sink in. The dealer's expression twisted into something like disgust and from a pained smile the man tried to voice something with choked scorn.

'What, is this Halloween now? What the fuck is this...?'

The target's hand moved toward a jacket pocket, but before the movement could be completed, his hand had flicked out, sending a projectile deep into the man's throat, and the first scream pierced the night air.

2

Detective Lieutenant Raymond Knight studied his new partner closely from the passenger seat of the unmarked Audi, as the younger man negotiated the down town traffic with the use of bitter curses and profanity. He could not quite decide if the arrival of detective Carl Brooks would make the job unbearable or just considerably more taxing, but the early signs were not encouraging. Responding to the notification over the radio with near gleeful enthusiasm, it was all Ray could do to keep the rookie's adrenalin in check with soothing noises and pray they avoided rear-ending someone at the lights.

Brooks was in his late twenties at most, with thick black wavy hair, and eyebrows to match. He handled the steering wheel like he was racing a kids toy, while his hulking frame tensed and flexed impatiently in the drivers seat, as if a wild bear had become trapped in the vehicle, looking for food.

Ray maintained a more relaxed composure, despite the toothpick swapping anxiously from one side of his mouth to the other; an equally bulky, but more compact, greying specimen, Knight had the neat, anonymous look of any professional. When people looked at him, the word 'policeman' did not come instantly to mind, and Knight maintained that deceit carefully.

To resist the craving to smoke, Ray always carried with him a pack of toothpicks, and would regularly bring one to his lips to chew on, to satisfy a long-time habit that still nagged at him, even now. Ray had promised his then-wife he would quit, if he made detective, and ten years later, he wondered why he bothered holding good to the promise as they hurtled along Ambrose Boulevard. A cigarette would be most welcome right now. He waited for the swearing to subside as Carl jerked the car to a near halt, to avoid running into the back of a commuter bus, then he raised his hand calmly to point to the bus lane opposite.

"Pull over there. You may be able to get this car down that alley, but we'll never get it out again."

They climbed out of the Audi and crossed to where the responding officers marked the entrance to the crime scene. The last of the light over Templeton was just surrendering to the neon and street lights of late evening, and a cold drizzle circulated constantly in the air, coating everything with a slick of moisture. This would likely continue well into the night and the next morning, if it did not develop into a full on storm. Ray zipped his jacket up under his chin and pulled a baseball cap tight over his head.

Nothing would keep out the chill.

A hot head, or some whizz kid, Ray tested the labels against the new man. Neither option appealed, he only hoped Brooks' 'newness' at least meant the man would be more likely to volunteer for some of the more dangerous and unpleasant work that might crop up; or, better still, tackle the paperwork. Any task that Knight found tedious, but would be 'good practice' for the rookie.

Whoever the man next to him turned out to be, Raymond had a pretty good idea why the Captain had assigned the young 'Go-getter' to him, and he smiled ruefully at the underhanded ploy. The offer of an early retirement would have been more effective; instead, Knight surmised he would have to pretend to be on his game for some while yet, and that would mean showing his face, signing the forms, and not making any mistakes.

He waited for Carl to flash his badge and then they ducked under the crime scene ribbon and proceeded down a narrow pedestrian walkway, their shoes splashing regularly in shallow pools as they proceeded. Carl was clearly itching to join the team clustered around the epicentre up ahead, but Ray observed how dark it had suddenly become.

Ray had lived in the city for thirty years now, ever since he had moved there from a small southern town to be with Karen, his wife. His ex-wife. In all that time, it had never failed to surprise Ray how, during the course of the job, he would discover some new, shadowy secret space, festering within the gleaming, grand facades of the city; A little crevice or enclave, hidden between the soaring towers and marble facias, among the maze of streets and infrastructure. There always seemed to be somewhere where nobody ever looked, some unknown, unloved spot, concealed by grime and squalor, that some unfortunate somehow managed to uncover, crawl into, and die.

And here was another such place. The neon forensic body suits were already scouring the greasy, pot-holed ground, picking through the litter and debris, and the nearest one to the interior barrier tape looked up and waved when he saw them. Ray nodded back and waited while the operative removed his face mask.

"Is that Ray Knight? Good evening, sir."

Ray smiled. "Marcus. What have you got for us?"

"I don't think you're gonna like this, detective." The forensic officer, returning the smile, indicated the lumpen form behind him, shrouded in a thin sheet of plastic, ready for removal. They had both been in the force for many years and long since become familiar with each other. Ray could care less how the other thought of him, but he was keenly aware that the information that Marcus could provide more often than not wrapped up most of the cases he was lumped with.

Ray glanced at his partner, to gauge the reaction to his first on-the-job murder, and saw Carl was keenly focussed. His eyes darted around the shadowy enclosure, hungrily. Ray, too, let his eyes roam around the scene.

The only real smell that Ray could notice was the familiar odour of decay coming from the rotting waste in the wheelie bins and a small skip under the fire escape stairs. Most of the blood must have been dispersed by the early morning down pour, as Ray could see none. There was a constant gurgling sound as several drains in the corners of the enclosure tried to cope with the influx of rainwater. He indicated the light coming from one of the back doors facing the alley.

"Do we know what we got there? Is it a

restaurant?"

Marcus shook his head. "The officer says its a small casino." The forensics man continued. "There's no sign of firearms, other than the one in the victims jeans."

"He clearly had no time to use it." Observed Carl.

Marcus glanced at Ray. "You got yourself a new buddy?"

"Yeah," Ray growled. "He's pretty green, and obviously very competent, as you can see. knives?' he asked, which received an affirmative nod. "Any I.D.?" he ventured, with little hope.

"Plenty,' the forensic man replied. 'His wallet was right there in the other pocket. With a neat little roll of cash as well.'

Ray's could not stop the low groan escaping from his throat.

'That's not the best of it, detective. I estimate there is at least half a kilo of heroin stuffed in his mouth. The wounds are minimal, but seem to be selected well to ensure fatality."

Ray swiped a hand slowly down the length of his face, slewing off the moisture there, and he stared down at the shape of the corpse with a dejected glumness. Agitated beyond any hope of patience, Carl manoeuvred himself into his partners eyeline and pitched his enquiry. "What are we saying, then? Are we dealing with a drug-related murder or not? Is this a gangland hit?" Ray just shrugged and shook his head slowly, then turned back to Marcus, who was not yet finished with the bad news.

"There's something else, I'm afraid. I think you better come take a closer look, the photographers have already documented most of it."

The forensics man led them closer to the corpse,

but pointed to a spot on the wall behind. Carl fumbled in his jacket pocket for a moment, before he produced a torch and shone it in the direction Marcus had indicated. That day's miserable weather had done all it could to obscure and erode the clarity, but on the masonry, picked out by the bright beam, it was clear there was some kind of image or graffiti, depicted in a dark pigment. It was about five feet in height, from what the roving focus of Carl's torch revealed. Ray squinted harder and tried blinking a couple of times, but eventually some meaning started to emerge from the shapes.

With an inquisitive glance, the forensics guy pre-empted the detectives question. "We believe it was made with spray paint, from a can. From the bleaching and dripping you can see it was fresh, from within the last twenty four hours. Not likely some bored kid tried to paint his masterpiece, but overlooked all this heroin and money..."

Ray took a quick stock count of the circumstances and went silent with the grim conclusion he came to. He let out his breath with a deep sigh and looked at Carl, who he could see had also been taking a moment to digest the new information. He was clearly having trouble putting it in order.

The image on the wall was a crude stick man, with four limbs splayed out either side of a single line torso, but what confused the effect was what surrounded the figure. It spread out from below the head and tapered back down to the where the legs began, and despite the haste with which it had been depicted and the erosion of rain water, it was still evident what it was supposed to be. They were wings.

Carl Brooks was unable to tolerate his partners

silence any longer, and over the patter, dripping and gurgling of the rainfall, which had intensified in the last few minutes, he asked loudly, “So what are we looking at?”

Ray took his time to respond, mentally sifting through the possible options, all with the common goal that Brooks would not want to hear. He glanced at the younger man and shrugged, then regarded the forensics man again.

“I will try get the report to you sometime tomorrow afternoon.” Marcus said.

Knight reached out to grasp the man’s shoulder, to emphasise his meaning.

“Take your time,” He said, slowly and clearly. *Enough so I can dig a hole deep enough this case will never see the light of day.*

3

The man had died at his hands, and he felt now liberated, as if the last of any doubts had been expelled from his mind. It had felt good to see the shock and fright in the man’s eyes slowly become dulled as death took him, and the power he felt invigorate his body as he stood over the condemned and watched. His limbs still tingled with the memory of the movements that had delivered that soul to the underworld.

Sat now in the safe place, the hive of his imagination, surrounded by all the tools and toys that he had collected and mastered, he reflected on his first kill. His next would be so much easier, and infinitely more satisfying. It had to be done just right, and he would have no need of special toys or technical aids. All he would require was the blade, sharp and strong.

He was assured by the success of the mission that he was indeed on the right path, and his destiny was his to forge; it was within his undertaking, as long as he remained brave and diligent. But it was only a minor step forward, and the reality of his excursions had to be taken care of as well. To truly progress, he needed resources, and the paraphernalia that was necessary to make him as formidable as he aspired to be; as he must become. He needed money, and the things that only came from money.

Living in this barren and unlikely fortress year after year, and commandeering funds from companies that would not miss them (at least not urgently) he had been able to amass a substantial figure in an offshore account, which he logged into now and looked for any change in the numbers performance, in their growth and depletion. He calculated how much he could safely move, what it could afford him, and initiated the transfer. False agencies and fund managers had so far kept his wealth concealed and beyond the realm of regulation, and he was satisfied that this was still the case. He then swapped monitors and activated the software that had become his trading outpost.

The game he utilized was called 'City Surfer', and

was a simple but immersive, world building simulation. The graphics were basic, and the text boxes crude, but the interactive and unregulated platform was open and broad enough to accommodate what he needed to do, and who he needed to do it with. Within minutes, he had appropriated a simple avatar – a young school girl stereotype, complete with twin pigtails – and had launched this raggedly pixelated version of himself over the sparsely rendered, generic cityscape.

When he found the neighbourhood he was looking for, he let go of his birthday balloon and dropped onto the curb beside a row of taxis and a squalid looking betting centre. One of the sponsors of the game was a gambling platform, and in real time, gamers could place and collect on bets from real-life sporting events. He had profited from this before, but this time, Pigtails walked past the shop, ignoring a couple knife-fighting in the alley behind.

She halted beside a pair of soap-box preachers and waited by the fatter, bearded one. Eventually, a text box opened at the side of the screen, and the cursor at the end of the words blinked in anticipation of further responses.

> **CAN I HELP YOU, LITTLE GIRL?**

> **I HOPE SO.** Pigtails could not exactly look at the preacher, as the pixels did not stretch to pupil manipulation. The two characters just stood side by side.

>**WELL, THE LORD WILL DELIVER, MY CHILD.**

> **I NEED GUNS**. Pigtails smiley face did not alter with conversation either.

> **AND FIREWORKS**.

> **YOU NEED AN AWFUL LOT OF POCKET MONEY FOR THESE TOYS SWEETHEART**. The preacher character had stepped down from his soap box

and was now facing the schoolgirl. The reply was blunt, but in accordance with the pairs established coda.

> DO I LOOK FUCKING POOR TO YOU?

*

A new day had not improved the weather, and the dark clouds above the city canopy mirrored Ray's mood. Parking his fifteen-year-old Toyota (proven reliability came with age in Ray's opinion) in his allocated bay in the garages beneath the building, Ray took the stairs to the second floor. The city's police force was housed in a fairly nondescript and discrete premises, near Templeton's centre and occupying four floors, but it did include a sweeping flourish of steps from street level to the main reception area. It was the more secretive rear entrance that most of the staff opted for on arrival.

Already at that early hour, he pushed open the door to a wall of heavy but hushed activity, a repressed mental swamp of overworked and overstretched staff. Ray took a route to avoid as many people as possible, and nods, waves and greetings were practically non-existent as he navigated the human traffic. Being well known and popular in this place was a benefit he could live without.

He flinched as he almost ran into Lieutenant Watkins, angling from his desk toward the coffee machine. The trace of a smile that was offered from his colleague looked distinctly condescending to Ray's eyes.

"Morning Ray, how's tricks?"

Go fuck yourself. The impulse to voice the thought was so strong, he was surprised when he heard himself reply instead "White with one sugar, thanks for asking." and made it sound suitably amiable.

He sank behind his desk, habitually averting his gaze from the heap of files and memos that was growing ever taller beside the telephone, and executed the ritual of booting up his computer. Logging into the live system, he searched through that morning's assignments, trying to pick out the key words that would indicate an easy detail. Ones which had 'case closed' all but branded on them. There was one recorded at six forty five which read 'suspect detained at the scene' and gave an address; almost certainly a 'domestic', in Ray's experience. And another which read 'bodies found' and gave an address of a convenience store which had potential. One with 'shots fired' and 'suspect at large' he quickly dismissed. The tiers of violence which Templeton offered up ranged from the deadly to the mundane, and Knight had honed his skills to determine one from the other.

Beside him, the huge mass of his new partner lowered into position behind a remarkably neat and empty looking desk. Knight mumbled a greeting from the corner of his mouth and hoped that would be the end of the exchange, but the excitement radiating from the younger man was impossible to ignore. He slowly swivelled his chair around an inch or two to regard the self satisfied grin and anticipation in Carl's expression, and lamented that his colleague was perhaps more of the eager beaver than a muscle-bound meat head. Eventually, Detective Brooks could contain himself no longer, and divulged that he had prepared a profile of last night's victim, the one in the back alley courtyard, and offered the older man a printed page which featured a small mugshot, in one corner. Ray scanned it quickly.

Paul Tyler. Forty two. Five feet four inches and one hundred and twenty pounds. Twice served time, first time for 6 months, second for one and a half years. Numerous offences, including theft, assault and robbery, drug trafficking. If he was affiliated with any narcotics agents as an information source, they were not included in this data file, Ray noted. He looked up at his partner, giving him his full attention as he folded his arms across his chest.

"So, detective Brooks, what's your analysis of our murder?"

Carl paused, no doubt persuaded that this was some kind of assessment of his capability, although really, Ray just wanted to assess how far in the dark his partner was, and if he could be convinced to drop the case entirely. Carl cleared his throat and regarded Ray with a serious expression.

"I think that it was either some kind of execution or retribution. There was no apparent money or theft incentive, but the victim was a known and established pusher; he had plenty of previous, and a history that goes back to the nineties."

Both he and Ray had enquired of the officers at the scene and of the few onlookers if there had been any sighting of anyone entering or exiting the alley. The neighbouring properties had also been quizzed, or what tenants had been available at that time in the afternoon. As yet, no witnesses had been found or come forward.

"I think the victim had known the killer, or had agreed to meet with him there. The motive appears to be revenge, or at least, the killer was trying to make a point."

Ray frowned as a team of officers began a debriefing in the breakout area behind them. Voices were raised and Ray leant in closer to partner. "What do you make of that tag on the wall behind the vic?"

Carl shrugged. "An identity tag? Are any gangs affiliated with the image? It must have meaning to the killer somehow."

Ray nodded in what he hoped looked like thoughtful agreement and sat back. The debriefing behind them was taking questions, and the phones were beginning to ring more frequently. It was only a matter of time before his would demand his attention, and that never ended well. He was running out of time to assign himself an escape route.

"Well, why don't you try filling in the report for last night, see how you get on. Take your time, paperwork is king around here, you gotta get used to it. I would just advise that you try not to be too conclusive at this stage, keep it..."

"Vague?" His partner offered, and Ray allowed himself a smile. *This guy may just be alright.*

Returning his attention to his email inbox, Ray's next priority was making sure he had no messages from the Chief, and was relieved to find only the standard daily notifications and reminders, claiming an urgency that would never be observed. He checked all of them for deletion, including one that read 'Racial sensitivity workshop'. One of the few perks of advancing age was the assumption that you were likely illiterate when it came to technology, and when it came to these awkward 'awareness training' sessions, he could justifiably plead ignorance. Just for good measure, he deleted the 'compulsory computer skills' message as well, and then prepared to leave for the convenience store which he had assigned himself.

As much as he dreaded the threat from city streets, he was far safer in transit, where the only way to reach him was by radio. And then he rarely picked up.

4

Officer Roberts reached the address eventually at three thirty in the afternoon. His day had been a predictable slog so far, and he hoped this call out would be the gentle calming of a nosey neighbour and the straight forward report that it sounded. A tragically youthful drug overdose and a painfully prolonged moving on of a half naked drunk had soured his morning to the point he was urging on the end of his shift already.

He had cause to be doubtful, however, as this was a fairly deprived area of the city, and he recognised the high rise from numerous call outs in the past. A colourless and functional block, designed for the multiple occupancy of those who could not afford anything else. Nevertheless, Roberts climbed the stairs briskly, noting with some pride his relatively steady breathing upon arriving at the fourth floor.

He heard the dog before he rang at the door to number forty eight. It was the kind of high, tortured whine that could only be interpreted as distress and alarm, as close to crying and sobbing as a canine could come. He was able to tell, from experience, that it was coming from a dog of no formidable size, and was likely a spaniel or other puppy. The noise was echoed by an infant, coming from an apartment on the floor below, and Roberts fancied he could also hear the raised voices of a domestic argument from one of the floors above. If you waited around these places long enough, he thought to himself, a law would be broken soon enough.

As predicted, the door to forty eight was answered by an elderly resident, a fearful looking woman who asked to see his identification from behind a door chain. Roberts could see behind her the flitting, dark shapes of cats. Lots of cats.

"Thank goodness you're here, officer, I thought no one was going to come and I would have to listen to that poor animal all through the night. it never stops. He's been crying since early this morning and hasn't let up yet. The poor thing. he woke me up, he did, and it takes me forever to get off to sleep..."

"You know the dog, that it's a 'he'?" Roberts asked, refusing to move as the woman opened her door wide, as if to invite him inside. For all the unopened boxes and pieces of furniture he saw piled up in her hallway, he doubted there would be any room for him.

"Oh yes, I don't know his name of course, but I remember seeing him come and go. Only a Yorkie, you see, officer. I knew he would be no trouble to my little ones..."

"And the owner, Mrs Jakes? Did you know your neighbours name?"

She admitted that she could not recall if the owner

of the dog had offered his name or not, but they had crossed paths in the elevator and hall. According to her, he was a nice enough man, if a bit quiet; helped her with her shopping on one occasion. Only moved in a short while ago. Roberts encouraged her to talk on with suitably affirming noises, while he looked around the premises and sized up the fire exit and other points of entry. If it was a heart attack, it was unlikely the paramedics could get here in time to save anyone, if it was not too late already. He did not want Mrs Jakes to become alarmed and get in the way of the clean up, however.

"Thank you for your assistance, madam," He said, after a long wait for a pause in her talking. "Can I ask you to remain in your room and lock your door, just until I can make sure everything is safe."

Leaving room forty eight, officer Roberts crossed to room Forty six, and paused there a moment to listen at the door. No voices or movement of any kind, only the pathetic whimpering and whining, and beneath that, a feeble scratching sound. He raised his hand and wrapped a knuckle on the door, calling out to the occupier of the apartment. As expected, there was no answer, and so Roberts thumped heavily on the door three times and called out clearly and firmly. The only effect this had was to silence thc dog.

Roberts braced himself to commence the task of kicking in the lock, hoping it was as aged and uncared for as the rest of the block itself, but to his surprise, the door to forty six opened at the turning of the handle. This immediately put the officer on edge, and he forced himself to open the door slowly and cautiously, reaching at his hip and removing the steel baton from its holster there. He leant into the apartment and called out again, slightly less firmly this time. His senses were straining to hear any noise or movement that came from inside, and his eyes quickly scanned for every door and every room to get a mental picture of the layout.

A small ginger shape darted out from around a door at the end of a short hall, and zipped between his feet and out into the lobby. It made Roberts jump and raise his baton quickly into the ready position. He breathed out heavily, while he told himself it was just the dog, then willed himself to move forward, in the direction of the room that the animal had come from. Before he reached it, he caught the familiar smell that every law enforcement officer came to recognise, and were trained to identify. He swallowed, realising the smell was coming from beyond the door in front of him.

It was gloomy in the apartment; the curtains had not been drawn back to let in the daylight. As Roberts pushed open the door to what was the bedroom with his foot, baton raised at his shoulder, a small lamp from the corner was the only light to illuminate the scene that met him on the other side. A sharp intake of breath, and he flattened against the wall closest to him, unconsciously seeking to distance himself from what he was looking at. Officer Roberts' day had just got a lot worse.

*

Another dead guy. This one was Asian in appearance, and covered in blood; a dinner plate-sized hole torn through his sweater and leaving the centre of his chest an open, gory void. His body lay on the shop floor, his flailing arms disturbing a display of soup cans. Streaks of blood decorated the counter front and up the shelves beside him, and toward the back, a separate smear of blood indicated where the shop owner had stood, and then sunk to his knees. Ray liked the look of this one, it felt straight forward, and he looked through the splintered mosaic of the shop window at the sole witness, crouched on the steps outside. She was being comforted by the responding officer, and in Ray's opinion, she looked teary and shaken, a sure sign that she would want to put this incident well behind her, and try her best to forget about it.

The poor guy who was working the counter that evening was being loaded into the back of an ambulance, and Ray hurried outside to the medic holding open the door. He nodded, flashed his badge, and asked if the guy looked like making a quick recovery. The medic assured him that he certainly would not be returning to work the next week, and Ray watched the figure strapped on to the gurney, breathing mask obscuring his face, and felt a chill go up the back of his neck. There were more dangerous jobs than his in this city.

That morning the weather was remarkably calm, which added to the general quiet and stillness that always followed a public shooting. It was as if the whole area were holding its breath, anticipating a resumption of the violence, and Ray glimpsed the odd face in a distant window, or figure peeking out from around a corner, curious to observe the aftermath. He returned to the officer and thanked him for taking care of the witness.

Wide, mascara-smeared eyes rose up to look into his face, and to Knight's irritation, she still had the presence of mind to ask him if there was anything else she could do. Ray assured her that her statement would be sufficient. "Let the officer take you home and try and get some rest." He said, then placed his hand on the officers elbow to angle him around and out of ear shot. Ray spoke softly, just above a whisper.

"She get a look at the second shooter?" When the officer shook his head, he continued. "She was scared, probably thought she saw gunmen springing out of every window. Let me handle it from here."

He had about thirty minutes before the crime scene analysts arrived, so he had to be quick. He looked closely at the nearest closed circuit television camera, mounted near the entrance, and followed the trail of the little cable leading from the back of the unit. To be sure, he did the same with another of the camera's behind the counter, but in the end, he was right. Often in these little local stores, the finances were so tight that it was common place for tradesmen to install cameras just for show. They were not circuited to any recording feed, and performed no function at all other than appearing to would-be burglars that there was a system installed. In the small store behind the counter, Ray found nothing but a kettle, some junk food and a laptop. There would be no video footage of what occurred.

Stepping closer to the shattered window, Knight could see the entry hole of at least two bullets, that most likely originated from a driver parked out front, waiting for the Asian man lying behind him to finish his business. When the shop keeper drew out the shotgun and complicated the matter, the driver had opened fire and then taken off at high speed, likely never to be found except after a thankless and exhausting investigation. Not on my watch, Ray swore to himself.

Tapping the edges of one of the entry holes with the end of his phone successfully dislodged a shard of glazing, that obscured any hint of a directed bullet. The exchange between the shop keeper and the robber were the culprits now, but following the direction of the escape driver's shot, Ray scoured the walls to finish the illusion. After about a minute of hunting, he located the tiny hole in the wall above the cigarette display cabinet. With the use of a pocket knife, he began to dig away at the hole, hoping that the brickwork behind had stopped what the thin plaster board could not, and after a minute more, had successfully retrieved the now rather squashed nine millimetre bullet. He took a moment to have a last look around, pleased with his morning's work, and grabbed a chocolate muffin off of the confectionery shelf, to compliment the takeaway coffee he still had in the car.

Robber holds up store; store keeper pulls out shotgun; fire is exchanged; end of. This case would be open and shut in an hour, and in the end, that was what the department really appreciated most. Everyone liked their violence simple and straight forward, not so much when it got out of control and messy.

5

Sweet justice! He could no longer imagine what had been so significant in taking another life, or why it could have cause to make him think anything of it. Nothing had stopped his hand that evening, and he had not hesitated in doing what had to be done. And if he were truthful, he had enjoyed it. Not that he had prolonged any pain or lingered on any torment, although he had every right to do so. He had simply proclaimed the judgement and delivered the justice, with cold, hard efficiency.

There had been much blood, and the subject had clearly suffered, but then, he had made it quite clear it was his due, and he was just performing the act of reckoning. It was more consideration than the man had deserved, and in his passing, his death would be one more marker in his glorious journey. A journey to a better world.

He had to confess a mild rush had clouded his senses, toward the end. A kind of triumphant verve, that quickened his hand and cleared his mind of all but the feeling of deliverance. It was a momentous occasion, and it was only natural that he should appreciate it. After all, he was performing a service for humanity, and one far more effective than the local city forces could ever deliver.

Especially that one, the policeman named Knight. What a worthless creature he had been, in comparison. What would that man have made of his actions, and, for that matter, what would come of their meeting, if their paths were to cross again? He wondered, as he returned the freshly cleaned and sharpened knife, in its place among the rest of his arsenal. What might he do, if he were to come face to face with detective Knight once more?

*

Raymond met Carl Brooks in the changing room, as he returned from his work out. The gym was located on the lower floor of police headquarters, and the officers were encouraged to use it, to maintain a minimum of fitness. Knight was there regularly, and not only to duck out of duties. He trained his muscles to help resist the ailments and niggles that many of his colleagues suffered from – the bad backs and shoulders and knees – but he was careful not to overdo it. Whereas, in contrast, from what he saw in glimpses at the man towelling down beside him, his new partner was evidently committed to growth. Bulges and fibres stood out and rippled as Brooks dressed himself, his breathing still fast and ragged.

"What were you training today, partner?" the younger man asked.

"Ah, just shoulders today. Don't like to go too heavy, just keep it slow, get the negative reps."

Carl smiled at him, clearly impressed. "Gotta go heavy on the shoulder press though, right? Anything under fifty kilos is a waste of time."

Some guys would never be content with how big they got, Raymond observed, and he wondered if his new partner was one of those guys obsessed with trying to be bigger and stronger than everyone else. "It's not always how much you do, but what you can do with it."

Carl laughed at this, and as both men prepared to leave the changing rooms, Ray changed the subject. "How did you get on with your assignment this morning?" he asked, and observed the note of uneasiness creep into the younger man's demeanour. Brooks had joined with Ian Fletcher on a shooting that had already been contained by the responding officers. A domestic incident, as Knight had rightly guessed, the girlfriend of the deceased had to be charged and escorted to the station. A relatively straight forward 'clean-up' assignment, Ray was still aware that emotional incidents like that could often be tough to manage.

Carl stiffened and squared his shoulders defensively. "I'll be alright. We did the charge sheet and she's in custody, but I bet you she'll go straight on suicide watch. Ian said he would close down the case."

"Good," Said Ray. "We get domestic shootings every other day around here. The ones involving children are the worst. They really stick in the throat."

Carl looked like he wanted to press the senior detective further on that matter, Ray could see the questions formulating in his creased brows, but thankfully Robert Carlson, a detective even older than Knight, spoke first as he joined them at the lifts. "You guy's get the notice?" Knight and Brooks both shook their heads and waited. "There's an emergency meet in the training hall. All available personnel. You better get your skates on fellas.'

The trio marched briskly out onto floor three, and when Brooks asked if they should bring a notepad or pen, Ray just scoffed. "Just make sure your face is visible and look concerned, like we've been there since the meeting began."

The headquarters training hall was normally an oppressively bare and quiet space that right then was packed to capacity, with a ring of bodies surrounding a few officers at the centre, who were busy around a couple of display boards. Ray recognised some of the crowd as beat officers and staff from other departments, and more than a few faces which he had never seen before. With Ray's broad shoulders and Carl's general size, they managed to muscle a route to the front where they adopted a suitably serious expression. It seemed to work, as the Captain turned round at that moment and his gaze hardly registered them at all.

Howard Watts was thinning gravely on top, and the remainder of his hair around the ears needed trimming. He was thick set but clearly overweight, and his face betrayed an age that could have exceeded his fifty eight years. Ray had always had respect for the Chief, if for no other reason that he came from a period when the drugs war had been a national concern, and the mafia were still clinging to power rather than portraying stereotypes in Hollywood movies. He was old school, but nonetheless, the man had that distinct commanding air of one who would tolerate no nonsense and that no one ever wanted to disappoint. Not if they valued their pension, that is.

Howard addressed the crowd in deep, gravelly tones. "I want you all to take a good look at the victim and look out for the file in your email. You know I wouldn't bring this to your attention if our guys hadn't identified at least one or two red flags that are concerning. Again, these details will be found in the files – read them. We are early on this one, and I want to shut it down before we have to call another one of these meetings."

Howard then stepped aside and indicated with his arms some of the photographs behind him. Everyone in the crowd scanned the images behind him with interest, but it was Ray and Carl who suddenly felt themselves rooted to the spot and gripped with a cold and uncomfortable prickling sensation. What was in the largest of the photographs was entirely unfamiliar, except for one aspect that struck them both, even from across the room. It was unmistakable, and it meant everything that Ray had been dreading. *'Oh, fuck, no.'* his first thought confirmed it.

The main photograph, enlarged to poster dimensions, showed a man in middle to late sixties, naked on top of a bed soaked through with blood. His body had apparently been mutilated, with wounds at the chest and crotch, and bound to the corner bed posts at each wrist and ankle with thin cord. His face was a pale nightmare of terror, and above his head, on the wall, was a very familiar image, smeared on the plaster in the man's own blood. A few straight lines, depicting a figure, with limbs splayed outward much like that of the victim. A figure, but at the shoulders great sweeps of blood extended outward, that were applied to illustrate only one thing; wings.

6

The press of the crowd packed closer in around the display boards, and Captain Watts had to speak over a general thrum of murmuring and low comments. He confirmed the timeline of the discovery of the body and gave a brief outline of the analysis from the psyche staff. Those few specialist recruits nodded their heads in affirmation and offered a few indicators that the photographs contained, which some of the younger officers were keen to take note of, as if there might be some exam on it later.

Carl took Ray's lead in not pushing forward with the rest of them, and despite numerous flashed glances, saw no sign that his partner was about to break his silence. A slump at his shoulders and the perpetual gape at his mouth were the only hints at his astonishment.

As Howard Watts reiterated his earlier command of reading the files and remaining vigilant, his general restlessness suggested the meeting had come to an end, and the staff of city headquarters began to slowly remove themselves from the room. As the numbers dwindled, Ray chose that moment to edge closer to the display boards, indifferent to the attention his behaviour was eliciting from the Chief of police.

Ray positioned himself about a foot away from the photograph of the victim, and remained there, scanning each pixel of the image with minute scrutiny. He frowned when he realised that what he was hoping not to see, was in fact actually there, and no amount of casual professional negligence would excuse his not seeing it.

"Something catch your eye, Raymond?" Howard Watts was no fool, far from it, and he was well aware of the rarity, and significance, of one his more 'seasoned' detectives taking an interest in a case not actually assigned to him. He hovered over Ray's shoulder, scrutinizing the man's face almost as thoroughly as the detective was scanning the photograph. Carl Brooks could not stand the tension any longer, and took great pains to clear his throat.

"Um, I think me and Ray may have something we need to discuss with you, Chief."

Watts did not look away from the senior detective and spoke out of the corner of his mouth. "So I suspected, detective Brooks. Perhaps you and detective Knight here better come in to my office. We can talk over it there, in private. If that's okay with you, Raymond?"

Knight had still not acknowledged his boss behind

him. He was finding it hard to tear his eyes away from the face of the victim. The harder he looked, the more convinced he had become. Not only were the signatures of this murder clearly aligned with the body of the drug pusher he and Carl had looked at two days before, but there was a whole other element that was apparent in the photograph that struck Ray a sickening blow. A realisation that not only opened up a sore memory or three, but reminded Raymond of a particular failure of his that had stuck in the back of his head for so long now he could not recall ever being free of it. This failure was now out in the open for all to see, and Ray blinked his eyes a couple of times in the hope his eyes were wrong.

He recognised the face of the man in the photograph. He knew the guy.

*

The loud rattle at the door promised the long-awaited delivery, and it took himself and both the two couriers to manoeuvre the great package into his domain. He tipped them well, as they were no ordinary delivery men, and their discretion and secrecy had to be assured. He signed for receipt, watched the truck leave, and then he closed the door and carefully began to peel off the cardboard and plastic wrapping. He was a little anxious, because he was not certain the item would answer his needs, but it had cost him a considerable amount of currency.

By mid afternoon, the device was fully assembled and ready for testing. He circled the object slowly, assessing its dimensions and making sure all the features were in place. Then, he retreated to the far end of the enclosure and took up the controller. Fingering the levers and buttons, he engaged the 'on' switch and observed as the twin pairs of propellers span into life, sending bubble wrap and bits of cardboard flying. With an eagerness he hoped was not rash, he attempted nudging the lever back a little, and looked in wonder as the whole chunky mass rose a couple of feet into the air.

A successful test and another good omen. Buoyed by the addition to his stockpile, he went to work on the overhead bars and pushed his already lean and muscular body to its limits once more. He slowly lifted, pulled and suspended his eighty five kilos into different stress positions and focussed on controlling his bodies response, coaxing his joints and ligaments to work in unison with his increasing strength.

He had already struck a blow for decency and he was almost ready to strike again, harder, and more spectacular this time. This was him now, who he was. Nothing would sway him from his mission, and he would show no mercy. It was too late for mercy. Like a white blood cell in a tainted blood stream, he would track down and attack any impure or toxic substance that threatened to corrupt the system. Nothing would escape him.

In the lull after his workout, and before he was due to commence an ordnance inspection, he crossed to his bank of desks and stopped before the tripod set off to one side. He adjusted the digital camera that was mounted there, and then took a seat positioned centrally in the lenses view finder. Checking the computer feed behind him to make sure he was correctly in shot, he touched a remote control to dull all the lights in the room. He then switched on a spot light at his feet, and started to read from a print out held in one hand, clearing his throat and starting again in different tones and pitches. Once this was completed, he revolved in his chair to face a computer monitor, and watched a playback of the recording he had just made.

He was satisfied. His next action was to access the browser that served his social media network and began to upload the images he had archived with the text he had prepared. His profile picture, from beneath the armoured headgear (that he had crafted to his exact specifications) provided just the right anonymity and intimidation that he desired, and lent his words the gravity that they deserved.

Before he logged back out, he clicked on an email notification in the side bar, from a contact he had been waiting on for several weeks. He read the list detailed within the message, and then sat back and allowed himself a pleased smile. The new information now on his hard drive was more than he could have hoped for, and he pondered for a moment on the appropriate malware he could use to act as the conduit for this data.

His efforts were finally beginning to come to fruition, and when eventually he revealed his identity, it would go hand in hand with the impact of his actions. **I will light a beacon for the spirit and the soul, and they will see this light as salvation. They must know it is me that will come for them, and they will fear my coming!**

7

The man in the photographs was Richard Darlow, sixty two years of age, unmarried and at the time of his discovery, subsisting off of welfare support. Able-bodied and generally of decent health, the reason Richard was living alone and jobless was because he had been released from a category D incarceration facility just six months before, where he had served eight years of a twelve year sentence for murder.

Richard Darlow had been a part time librarian and school teaching assistant, but became the main suspect in a string of sexually motivated killings involving young boys begun in the late nineties. He had been stopped on the highway for driving with a broken headlight, and on inspection of the boot of the vehicle, the officer at the scene had taken Darlow to the station for the suspicious items observed within that boot. One item had been a pair of handcuffs, and another had been a long, serrated and oddly-stained hunting knife. Shortly after arrival at the station, Mr Darlow's clear agitation and not-so-clear recollection of his comings and goings lead him to be detained for further questioning and his car impounded, and by the second day of custody, the homicide department were certain they had their killer.

The problem was, there had been at least half a dozen killings attributed to the child murderer and little in the way of hard forensic evidence. Moreover, Richard Darlow was no mentally deranged maniac, and quickly employed the services of a competent lawyer. Time was running out for the department to put their case forward, and they were only really prepared to convict on one of the murders – the most recent one – for which they had accumulated sufficient evidence to be certain of a guilty verdict. Although a successful conviction and a potentially long sentence was practically guaranteed, the department was reluctant to leave the remaining murder victim cases unclosed, and Mr Darlow's lawyer was well aware of this. Some of the body's of those previous victims had yet to be recovered.

After a heated conference, a decision was made to offer Richard a somewhat reduced sentence, on the condition he confessed to killing the other victims. He was also to provide the police with the location of the missing bodies. After a much shorter and less heated conference, Richard Darlow agreed to give the police what they wanted, and in time to take it all to court in orderly fashion. It was considered the best outcome by many, under the circumstances, but not by all, including one of the newly-promoted detectives working the case, Raymond Knight.

He now stood before his Chief of police, recounting the facts of the case and their discovery in the back alley courtyard, in a suitably sombre tone. He responded to the short, whiplash queries that occasionally interrupted his flow with common procedural excuses that every seasoned policeman had on standby.

Lying was something one mastered with practice and experience, and his performance so far was fairly convincing, he felt; almost as if he had been subconsciously rehearsing this moment for the last decade. He had planted his feet solidly apart, and set his shoulders squarely upright, by clasping his hands behind his back, to absorb all the mental beating his boss administered. His partner stood back a little, near the rear corner of the office, and watched with some admiration as the older man stood his ground.

"And you didn't think to flag his release, Knight?" Howard asked him now, clearly just shy of outright fury. Ray tried to make the point that a decade was a long time on the job, and with a glance at the rookie, he weighed up the advantages of placing some of the blame on the kid's inexperience. A problem shared was a problem halved, after all, but could it be enough to save his job?

"What about the pusher? You didn't flag up the signs there that the case was unusual?" Ray opened his mouth to reply, his gaze never wavering from the middle distance, when Brooks cleared his throat in the background and tried to offer an explanation. Watts barked him down, but noted with interest that the new guy was willing to back up his partner. Maybe he had made a mistake putting him under Knight's wing; the idea was to invigorate Knight's performance, not dilute the promise of the rookie. More annoying, Howard had the feeling he was becoming more ruffled in reverse correlation to Raymond's ease under fire, and eventually he had to get up from his desk in frustration and begin pacing around the office.

"We got the coroner's report this morning. I was going to file the crime scene report after that,' Ray lied. "In light of the new info, we can liaise with whoever you assign to Darlow and take it forward from there." Ray's throat was getting dry, but he could not afford to let his bravado slip. With any luck, Watts would lose it and kick them off the case entirely. *Step carefully, soldier,* he thought. *You want to bring this to the boil but you don't want him to explode.* But as Ray watched, the Captain seemed to nod and chew at his lip with a contemplative fervour which he did not like the look of. Howard Watts was coming to a decision, and the reduction in his pacing lapsed into a rigid flex up and down from the heels. He squared up to Raymond and spoke directly into his face.

"You know the operator in that district?" By operator, the Captain meant the most prominent figure of the local organisation affiliated with drug trafficking and general vice. Ray swallowed before he slowly nodded his head. Watts went on. "Meadows, isn't it? Yeah, that's our man. Why don't you drop by his place and run that pusher by him, see if he recognises him, or has any beef on our wingman."

Ray could not stop himself grimacing queasily. It was his turn to begin losing his cool. "I would have very little hope that he could provide us with any kind of insight, Chief, or even grant us an audience for that matter." Too beggy. He was losing ground, and Ray could tell he his boss was becoming more resolute.

"Maybe our guy has struck before, Knight, Who knows? Worth seeing what Meadows makes of it, and besides, he won't be wanting this killer on the street any more than we do."

Carl this time, clearly getting caught up in the excitement. "Is this guy head of a drug outfit? Will we actually have to bring him in?" Ray swung round on him with a contemptuous snarl. "Forget that, the man's a fucking psychopath. We'd have to have a case on him a mile thick before we'd have the balls to bring him in."

Howard looked pleased that he had gotten a reaction at last. "Good then, that settles it."

Knight could feel his core instinct of self-preservation being fatally compromised, and he did not like it one bit. He tried appealing on a first name basis, "Nothing could possibly come from kicking that hornets nest, Howard, 'cept maybe getting one of us killed."

"Are you refusing orders, Knight?" Ray averted his eyes back to the floor, and resisted any reply by furiously clenching his jaw. “Good. Get your files over to Jameson’s team for a sniff ‘n’ share, then despatch to Meadows before five. He should be awake and receiving guests about that time.”

He aimed a gruesome ghost of a smile at his boss before turning to exit the office. “We’ll be sure to wipe our feet and bring a bottle of bubbly, compliments of the division.” Knight hissed.

Carl Brooks took his partners lead in exiting, but did not share any of his morose despondency. He circled toward the Captain’s desk, on his way to the door. “Does this mean we are on the case, Chief? Darlow’s killer, along with Jameson?” A kind of loud cough combined with a groan came from the doorway, as Raymond tried to make it palpably clear that it was time to leave. The contrast in the two seemed to amuse the older chief of police.

“Brooks,” said Howard Watts. “D’ya see now why I doubled you up with Raymond? So you could see how the job should NOT be done.”

8

Dominic Lowe, eleven, bright and well liked at school. His mother had fussed over his hair and clothes, his father had gently pushed him into all sorts of sports and extra-curricular clubs. His photograph radiated good will, the vitality and promise of life, and as Ray gazed at it, all the old feelings of rage and resentment came back to him. And frustrated impotency. He had been strictly indoctrinated into his senior partners methods, and the Chief at the time had been coldly pragmatic. The media had gotten wind of the case fairly late on, and had tried to make up for it by documenting the arrest and trial of the suspect religiously. Raymond had suggested giving Darlow whatever he wanted, and then hang him out to dry in court; after all, the man had used all kind of lies and deception to lure his victims to their doom, why could they not behave likewise, he reasoned. This had been rejected out of hand – the law must be observed – and Ray had been made well aware that he was to observe proceedings only.

Worse, the duties allocated to him were handling the traumatised parents, delivering the knock-out blow they had all been dreading. It was up to him to inform them the light of their life had been snuffed out, and to be the caring face of the force as those parents broke down into inconsolable grief. Ray still felt uncomfortable when he recalled the parent of one child discovered toward the end of the investigation; the father had died previously of cancer, and her son was the only person that she truly cared about. She had paled immediately as she recognised him, stood on her doorstep, and when Ray had broke the news to her she had gone into a kind of catatonic trance that none of Ray's questions or sympathies could prompt her out of.

Ray had felt he had been made a kind of patsy in the Darlow case, and he suspected it was occurring again that day, as he listened to Jameson - *greasy, oily, numbers-man prick!* - discuss the data points, outline his strategies and generally take charge of everything. He tried to distract himself by mentally calculating the years and months until he could take retirement, but the figures were still daunting.

Ray more than ever needed to escape that building, get out in the open air and put some distance between him and the last twenty four hours. He needed to immerse himself in the chill, indifferent and troublesome real world, to escape from his thoughts and forget he was working for the Templeton police department for a while.

Usually when Ray wanted to get away from it all, he was drawn toward a mobile catering van that he had discovered over the river, near the waste recycling centre, and, under the pretext of 'grabbing a quick lunch', he allowed his old Toyota to guide him there now. The view of the city was not terrific, and it was not exactly the best side of town, but Ray liked the sound and sight of the water. It soothed him. A natural expanse of something other than concrete, that could not be crowded and tainted by man kind.

The snack van was run by an old Greek, who had settled in the country many years ago, and to Ray's eyes, could be anywhere from forty years of age to seventy. He had a weathered look that he wore well, and he smiled when he saw Ray and raised a hand.

“Hello, my fren’. How’re you today?”

“Still breathing, Yanni, thanks for asking. How’s business?”

The Greek grumbled something about the weather and finished serving his customer before asking Ray if he would like his usual. Ray ordered, and then perched on a bollard beside a cobbled brick slipway leading down to a narrow jetty, watching the grey churning flow of the Dunster's current.

Sea birds squabbled and dived over the swell that afternoon, taking a break from scavenging human waste, and Ray looked out at them, blowing and sipping at a hot chocolate and taking bites from his chicken wrap. As usual, his mind drifted back to his child and her mother, and he wondered for the hundredth time if he had chosen a different career they might still be together. And, if they had remained together, would he be a happier person for it?

Instead, he had the child killer, Richard Darlow, so soon after being released, back on the departments desk. One of the last, most selfless and powerful compulsions he had remembered feeling was an urge to kill the man, and Darlow had not even wronged his family. What if he had killed his daughter, what would he do then? If Ray had been looking at a photo of Catherine in the murder files, instead of the Dominic Lowe boy?

The daylight was beginning to wane, and Raymond screwed up his litter and wished Yanni a fruitful evening before returning to his car. It had been a particularly shitty day, Ray lamented, but he was certain it was about to get a lot worse. With a wary reluctance, he stared at the car's glove compartment before compelling himself to reach over and fish out the object from inside.

In his lap, he glared down at the small, darkened steel revolver. The old detective special thirty eight was so small he could almost forget having it. His Sig Saur service pistol, a monstrous nine millimetre hand cannon, remained locked in its case in his desk, where he preferred it. He felt less secure with it around. These days, if a law officer used deadly force, it seemed the chances were he would likely be charged with murder and be the one to face jail time. This scared Ray more than someone actually shooting at him. He was of the opinion that if an investigating detective had to discharge a weapon, then there must have been a serious breech of procedure somewhere. The gun squad were on stand by for lethal confrontations, it was their job.

He marvelled at the heavy little lump in his hands, and also how unsure he was of how to operate the action. He pushed at a button that looked likely, then when that did nothing, he pulled at it, and the cylinder swung out from the frame of the revolver. Ray squinted at the five circular brass ends of the live rounds, all loaded with the explosive to deliver the metal bullets at a lethal speed. He carefully pushed the cylinder back into place until it clicked home, and asked himself if he had ever cleaned this weapon. If it had never been fired, did he need to? Ray resisted the temptation to turn the gun in his hands and stare down the barrel. Instead, he placed the deadly little tool into his jacket pocket, draped over the seat beside him. He recalled somewhere, perhaps from a movie he had seen once, that in an emergency, he could fire the gun from inside the pocket, and take his adversary by surprise. Ray was satisfied for the time being to try and just forget again that it ever existed, started the car's engine and pushed it into gear.

9

The man felt comfortable on the streets, but at the same time detached from what he observed around him. He could return the gaze of any street corner dealer or trouble maker, confident they would recognise in him the same resolute anger and capacity for violence. Eager predators, they could circle one another and keep a respectful distance, senses alive at all times for that perception of fear, of blood in the water. They understood one another, were wary of one another, and the man journeyed past them protected by the shield of shared discontent and mischief. He was bound for what he considered to be the breeding ground for all this sub-human trash, a classification that he would not share with them. He was a cleaner, he cleansed the streets of this trash; dragged it out into the open, and disposed of it. To him, it was the natural order of things, or would be soon enough.

The people of the city, ignorant and indifferent to the hazardous squalor around them, they did not register to the man. The weak and the potential prey of this circling depravity, the man was aware of them only as a man may be concerned for his hunting dogs. They were often first to encounter the danger, and their howls and yelps would alert him to his quarry. If someone fell victim to one of these predators, and they were in his audio range, then he would act fast, and act decisively, ruthlessly.

He was coming closer to the hub of all the disease

and rot in the city, the main den of the depraved. It was here that he knew that he would find the ultimate test of his courage, and the supreme test of his dedication. If all his training and reading and preparation had been worthwhile, if he was truly on the right path and acting upon a force that was greater than he could conceive, then he would pass this test and transcend to the level he knew that was necessary. He was set upon wreaking havoc and destruction, and by the end of this evening, the only outcome would be the fall of his enemies, or the sacrifice of his own life.

*

Slowing the Toyota as he rounded the central roundabout onto Westgate street, Ray quickly noticed the big, broad-shouldered form of his new partner, waiting patiently beside a small snacks kiosk. When he saw Ray, the man's expression shone with a wide smile and Carl Brooks approached the car with boyish excitement. Ray shook his head and scowled in wonderment. *He's actually looking forward to this fucking ordeal*! The thought lowered his estimation of the younger man down a notch or two, but Carl was clearly unaware of his partners disapproval as he leant into the Toyota's Lowered window, and greeted the senior man cheerfully.

'Where you been, Gov?'

'Never you mind, muscles. Let's just get this shit-show over with shall we?'

'Not in this heap 'o shit we ain't. We take the Audi or you're going alone'

Ray quickly weighed up the pros and cons of that

one, but his partner had already opened the driver side door. In the end, the price of petrol swayed the older man, and the fact that the Audi could reach much higher speeds more quickly, in the event that they might have to beat a hasty retreat, was also a strong factor. He climbed into the more modern car and let his partner take the wheel.

Slowing at a set of lights, Brooks turned to his passenger. “Ian Fletcher told me you still carry nothing but an old Smith, is that right?” Carl asked

Ray’s hand instinctively moved to the bulge in the right pocket of his jacket. “What of it?”

“I thought we all had to practice with the Sig? Fifteen bullets is a lot more than five or whatever shit you got packing there.” Carl, still rolling up to the red, drew out his semi automatic. “Nine millimetre is considered the minimum calibre for stopping an assailant. I’d prefer to be packing the ten mil’ myself.”

Ray winced. A muscle-bound meat head he could handle, but a gun nut to boot was too much. It was hard enough to maintain a healthy distance from the crime and violence on the streets, but it became much harder still if you were lumbered with someone who raved over their firearm and were itching for excuses to use it. Carl Brooks had just become another liability in Ray’s mind.. It was hard to keep the annoyance out of his voice when he replied. “If I ever need your help, then by all means, you come in blazing with the Sig. And a flame thrower, if necessary. I’m not carrying one of those, either. In the mean time, please keep your piece concealed, detective. Criminals tend to get nervous around guns.”

The Dunster bridge ended on a rise in the city’s geography, and Blackbrook estate lay beneath the great concrete footing of that landmark. In perpetual shadow of the freeway exit overhead, Blackbrook may have once been an important stop in the river's industrial past. Now, it simply smeared the far eastern bank of that district of the city, and no planners had ever decided what to do with it; either develop and modernise, or tear down and rebuild. A compromise of the two had never been attempted, and in the end, it occupied its own darkened territory, largely ignored and forgotten. As predicted by many of the lingering tenants, the whole area swiftly succumbed to crime and lawlessness. Few police officers dared patrol this close to Blackbrook, and there was a shared dread among response units to ever be called out to the place.

Ray directed his partner away from the civilized centre of the city, but his instructions reduced to low growls of '… left here...' or '...turn there...' as it became all too apparent that they were nearing the cursed grounds. The background song of ambulance sirens was rarely absent and the ageing, grime-ridden architecture betrayed a neglect that seemed to extend to the tenants of the faceless apartment blocks.

What people they saw shambled nervously out of plain view or hugged the shadows. The only people that looked their way, instead of pretending to be blind to their arrival, were the handful of ladies that lingered under the street lamps at the head of the side alleys and lanes. Nameless businesses operated out of makeshift voids of brick and timber, several letters missing in their neon titles, either by crooked wiring or by vandalism. The whole place, like its inhabitants, was very much unloved and unlovely.

In the passenger seat, Ray stewed silently in the dark unpleasant soup of his own thoughts, chewing on a toothpick, and staring out of the window. Keep moving, that was all that Ray thought life boiled down to. As he observed the remnants of a society, of the people left behind and excluded from the prosperity of civilisation, he reasoned this was a fair summation. You stop swimming, you die, and as the car slid past the empty shells of buildings and broken shards of phone boxes and traffic signs, he came to see the human race as so many fish, with sharks swimming among them. Predators and prey, and while the majority of the population were unwittingly classed as prey, the man they were due to meet that evening could only be classified as a predator. Shaun Meadows cruised through the filthy shallows of life, picking off the weak, snapping at those that got too close, and in his tow, smaller specimens clung to him for protection. Small-time dealers, pimps, traffickers, groomers and killers; all disposable, all feeding off the scraps and crumbs from Meadow's jaws. Could their man, the corpse in the back alley courtyard, be one of these parasitic hangers-on?

Their car pulled up beside an empty and darkened road. Only one in every three street lamps appeared to function, and if any parking restrictions were applicable here, Ray guessed that they were rarely enforced. An old Honda on the other side of the road, with a smashed-in rear window, had tyres so flat the vehicle rested on its hubs. He doubted if it had been driven for years.

At the corner of the road, the two detectives arrived at a three storey, 1930's style, brown-brick building, much like many of the others in the area, except this one was alive with exceptionally loud rap and grime music. Looking up at the windows running around the entire perimeter of the third floor, which was where Ray suspected that Shaun Meadows actually resided, it was lit dark blue like some chill out lounge of a late night club. As they stood before the entrance, a couple of youths tumbled out of the doorway and staggered down the shallow steps to the pavement beside them, apparently oblivious to their presence, and insensible with constant giggling.

Ray's eyes roamed forlornly over the whole massive facade, as if he were looking at his own tombstone, then he called over to his parter, above the din of the music, "Welcome to paradise!"

10

Two suitably massive guardians, probably packing armoury many times more effective and deadly than their own, studied the pair of detectives intently, sizing up their bearing and garb and reaching an accurate conclusion.

"What you want here, copper? You're a long way from the police station you know."

Ray cleared his throat. "I believe Mr Meadows is expecting us? An acquaintance rang earlier and made an appointment."

An appointment? Carl's quizzical look said to Ray, who shook his head inconspicuously to discourage any objections, but the words seem to have their effect. After a brief exchange into a mobile phone, the two doormen stood aside, like a canyon forming within a mountainside, and the two detectives were led to what had to be some kind of communal lobby. There were a few, cheap, cinema-style plastic seats at the far end, and they were invited to sit with the brusque wave of a hand. Here, they could observe a messy rabble of young men and women, engaged in various leisurely pursuits.

There was a pool table near the centre of the space, where, in between shots, the players would lean on their cues and stare over at them suspiciously, from within a thick, hanging fog of tobacco smoke and an aroma of something more exotic than tobacco. An array of armchairs around a large television screen attracted much more noisy attention as a half dozen guys waged brutal combat within some virtual computer game. Weaving around these two arenas were several striking looking woman, all in very provocative attire, who lounged and leaned against the furniture, secreting glances in the detectives direction. There was even a small bar located in the corner, which appeared to employ a serve-yourself policy.

It could all have appeared relatively innocent, were it not for the tell-tale bulges, butts and barrels of handguns that were visible in many of the pockets and waste lines of the guests in that lobby, and Ray and Carl made their own assessments on which of them looked most likely to draw and potentially use their weapon. With a nudge and a nod, Ray indicated the fire doors and windows that he thought may make the best emergency exit if they had to beat a hasty retreat, but for the best part of ten minutes, the pair just sat and waited as calmly as they could pretend to.

Ray tried to isolate and identify the different accents he detected, counting Russian and North African among them, but quickly felt the drawn out passage of time wearing thin on his nerves. This was one of the last places on Earth he wished to be, and the noise and the laughter and spying eyes were beginning to increase his heart rate and make his foot tap out a manic rhythm on the floor. He looked sideways at Carl, and saw the big man was looking down intently at his smartphone, occupied with whatever he had found to scroll through on the tiny screen. He looked unmoved by the situation, and in fact, to Ray's incredulity, he stopped one of the passing gang members and ask them for the WiFi password.

Ray slipped his hand into a jacket pocket and retrieved another toothpick; he had chewed the last one to atoms. If the worst came to worst, he thought to himself absently, he could stab someone in the eye with the other end.

Eventually, one of the entrance sentinels returned, and indicated for them to get up and follow their lead. They were grateful to leave the cinema seats, on exhibition as they were, but still Ray felt stiff and awkward as they were marched past the loafing crowds and into a darkened corridor beyond. They were met by another two large, imposing looking foot soldiers, who indicated for them to open their jackets and hold out their arms. A quick nod from Ray, and both detectives complied, and finding their badges and little else, they were approved to continue. No issue was made of Carl's service pistol or Ray's revolver, which made him think they had been considered so inconsequential as to not be worth worrying about. He could not decide if it was a good thing or bad thing if these people figured them to be harmless, despite being technically armed.

All five of them then slowly marched to a lift that opened after one of the foot soldiers stabbed at a button on the keypad beside it. Without ceremony, they all squeezed in, and the restricted space inside just barely contained there combined mass. There they stood, rigidly determined to not make eye contact with one another.

Enclosed away from the noise of the crowds and music, an ominous silence descended on the party as they rose upward to the next floor of the building. If anyone was feeling the oppressive mood, not one of the grim, stony expressions on the men in that lift showed it. Ray tried to keep his shoulders square and his back straight, commanding the space his body required to fill, but he was nonetheless acutely aware of the semi automatic rifle butt cradled in the arm of the man to his right, which was almost resting on his shoulder. His eyes flicked upward briefly. *One more hour, just give me one hour. After that time, we'll be gone and far away. Just be on it, keep it together, stay calm...*

*

The time had arrived. He was in place and his quarry had been sighted. The long evening of observation and preparation had culminated to this point and he had to be ready. It was do or die time.

His tools were laid out beneath him and his suit was fastened and secured. The evening air was chill and refreshing against his body, and the rain had lifted to maximise visibility. Everything was as it should be, and in that moment he was elated with a blissful satisfaction. Many years hard work and mental transformation had brought him to this place, at this time, and he now sensed that he was being truly guided, as if he was being utilised by some more powerful and omnipotent force.

A thousand lights were blinking on up and down the towering monoliths of distant buildings, like stars on a vertical sky. Advertising screens and intricate digital branding glittered into being like concentrated super novae, and the man beheld his universe, feeling like a god looking down on his celestial galaxy. Nothing else mattered right then but that feeling.

A final inspection of the equipment, a tighten here, a tug there, and he got into position. His muscles tingling with anticipation, he flexed his thighs, took a quick breath, and kicked off, into the air. The rush of air was exhilarating, and as the wind filled his wings and slowed his fall, he could almost believe that this was what it felt like to fly.

11

Coming to a stop on the second floor, the doormen exited, while the remaining two gang members indicated for Carl and Ray to wait. One of them pushed at the door button inside of the lift, and they all waited for the lift to continue to the third floor. They continued to wait for the lift doors to slide shut, and the same man pushed the door button again, but just then, the enclosure began to shake violently and a mighty rumble assailed everyone's ears. All four men desperately tried to steady themselves to prevent being rocked off of their feet, and as loud thuds and bangs came from above them, presumably from falling debris, they as one elected to scurry out onto the second floor and take up position against the wall, looking around in bafflement.

A second enormous concussion followed within seconds, once more making the entire building tremble beneath their feet. This removed all doubt the occurrence was a freak one off, and the two foot soldiers both raised their rifles, sliding back the bolts as they did so. They instinctively sidestepped into a back-to-back stance, covering each end of the long second floor corridor with a gun barrel.

Ray and Carl glanced at each other, to see the look of shock mirrored in the others eyes, and then refocussed on their two escorts, to observe what they would do next. It was dark on that floor, with no illumination but for an old strip light embedded in the ceiling tiles, but there was nothing really to see except for the less expansive and empty lobby area opposite and the long row of doors, stretching away either side into the far ends of the corridor. One or two of these doors began to sneak open, to give a glimpse of alarmed eyes in attractive faces. From what he could see, these ladies were not entirely dressed, and Ray guessed that a lot more than just karaoke was practised in the rooms in this part of the building. The two foot soldiers shouted at the women, waving their arms frantically, and the faces disappeared back inside.

Ray saw Carl's hand begin to creep inside his jacket, seeking the semi automatic pistol, but Ray caught his eye and shook his head firmly, prompting Carl to halt the action. The situation was precarious enough without the rookie thinking he was in some kind of Hollywood action movie. The four of them did nothing more then breath heavily, the rifle barrels of the two soldiers held steady out in front of them, but rising and falling with every breath. They waited, and Ray squeezed his eyes tight shut in an effort to get his heartbeat under control.

Then they heard the first sounds of gun fire. This was joined by the barely audible sounds of raised voices, which soon increased in volume, until it became apparent they were listening to people yelling and screaming. The bursts of rapid gun fire were underpinned by a more regular and constant boom of single round discharges, so it was clear that many different fire arms were being deployed. Combined with the many different pitches of yelling and shouts, it sounded like nothing less than open warfare. Some kind of major battle had erupted, and it was becoming obvious that the noises were getting closer.

A flicker, followed by a strobing blink, and the power feed to the lighting system snapped off. A second of total darkness, and a surge of panic, was alleviated only partially by the activation of the emergency backup system, which illuminated everything murkily from small red bulbs implanted high up the walls. It was then the fire exit doors burst in, and the air was filled with full-volume shouting and the cacophonous thunder of fresh gun fire.

Men came at a run, spraying bullets in the direction they had come from, and one of the foot soldiers tore off to intercept them, his companion left hopping from foot to foot in indecision. When the fire doors from the opposite end of the corridor burst inward, chaos successfully reigned over all. The foot soldier abandoned his guard of the two detectives, intercepting the men coming from the lower floor, who had come determined to enter the fray. There was an immediate danger that this raucous and heavily armed posse were about to collide with the heavily armed men trying to escape the battlefield coming from the floor above, and stuck directly in the middle, Ray and Carl hugged back against the wall watching this all play out, wishing they could melt into the plaster and disappear.

The situation was as desperate as Ray could ever have conjured up in his worst nightmares; the way out, clustered as it would be with fleeing gang members with loose trigger fingers, was as dangerous as the way ahead, with unknown gang members engaged in what sounded like more focussed and directed slaughter. His eyes rolled in anguish at the predicament he had been forced into, and Ray damned and cursed everyone he had ever known, in a steady stream of hissed and spat-out expletives.

He clawed at the lump inside his jacket pocket and drew out the small Smith and Wesson revolver. The five round cylinder suddenly felt very small and inadequate, in the immediate circumstances, but the hardwood grips felt solid in his palm and gave him something to grip to, as his mind raced. Various ugly scenarios of his demise came to him suddenly and vividly, which he tried to invert to find a possible path for survival. He looked at the tiny handgun, poised ready at his shoulder, and licked his lips in dread at having to pull the trigger. If that should occur, then the likelihood of return fire was very high, and in the present company, that would mean almost certain death. He glanced at Carl, and saw he too was gripping onto the butt of his Sig Saur, legs braced, and searching around for some means of escape.

The air of chaos heightened as the dull red gloom was regularly lit with lightning flashes of spent bullets, and the corridor began to reek of cordite, gun powder and smoke, some of it spilling down from the floor above. There must have been at least two or three dozen gang members, all jostling for space and yelling desperately into each others faces, uncertain of exactly where the threat was coming from and who to aim their firearms at. Ray grasped at his partners elbow, and when he felt his face near, he shouted above the din. “Now is not the time for heroics, if these fucks want to kill each other, let them get on with it,” he pointed toward the lobby opposite. “We need to get our heads down and call the cavalry. Now! Keep your gun arm down and for Christ sakes, do not try to shoot at anyone. These guys are just itching for an excuse to kill someone.”

As one, they left the sanctuary of the hard supporting wall, and charged forward with guns pointed at the ground, shouldering past bodies to leave the corridor and enter the lobby area. Here, there was only a small reception, store cupboard and a kitchenette, but Ray found a dividing wall that separated the lobby from a tall cabinet of mail boxes and an old style, broken-looking public phone.

They dropped into a crouch, and ears and eyes fixed on the melee beyond, they both regained their breath and wiped at the sweat collecting on their brows.

Ray dug out a mobile handset and dialled for the department, his lips working to remember the numbers for the call code for officers down and needing assistance. Carl racked the slide of the semi automatic and for the third or fourth time checked the manual safety was off. Ray's eyes squinted shut in the effort to contain his panic and dutifully recite the information the operator required to complete the transfer. When an officer came on the line, he barked out the address, twice, and gave the response code.

Ray turned to Carl, and recognised the manic gaze of someone torn between fight over flight in the adrenalin-fuelled decision that every animal, hopelessly cornered, was forced to make. Their situation hang in the balance, and as much as Ray would have liked to flee madly in the first direction that came available, he knew the prize of survival would only be won right then by rational thinking and proceeding with caution. And with luck.

"Carl, we have to keep our heads, alright? Its gonna take time for the troops to get despatched and even longer for them to reach us, so we're gonna have to rely on each other to get out of this, you understand?" His partner nodded mutely, and Ray prayed the meat head would not lose it and start emptying the Sig at anyone he saw. "Now, I don't think we can get out by strolling through the front doors, not now. It'll be Armageddon down there, and I don't fancy our chances waiting here."

Ray shifted sideways to peep back around the wall, as he reviewed in his mind the option his own words were leading to. He gnashed his teeth in exasperation. "Fuck, Carl, I think we're gonna have to go on, get up, maybe, on to the roof?"

This time his partner found his voice, and Brooks gave Ray a twisted grin. "We came here to find Shaun Meadows, lets go fucking find him and have a chat!"

Ray coughed out a short, ironic laugh. "We can tell him how disappointed we are with his hospitality!" But any merriment was doused by a sudden fresh burst of machine gun fire, several rounds clunking into the metal of the mail boxes above them. *One fucking hour, that's all I fucking asked for!* Ray thought, bitterly.

12

The gun fire became less frequent, more speculative, and the figures that emerged from within the smoke now staggered and limped from injuries and wounds. At Raymond's suggestion, Carl got up and took the lead away from their hiding place, and in his head, Knight tried not to calculate the odds of a bullet hitting the younger man's giant frame prior to his own. If he could save the kid as well as his own skin, then that would be a bonus.

As Brooks advanced down the corridor, one of the straggling gang members goggled in panic at the sight of them and raised his piece to aim it in their direction. The two detectives, pointing and shouting over the barrels of their firearms, convinced the youth to abandon the notion, drop his rifle and scurry away. Emboldened slightly by this minor success, they continued down the corridor, step by careful step.

The stairwell beyond the fire exit doors was like some bleak parapet from some hellish, spooky castle. It was lit only by the emergency red lamps behind embedded iron grills, and clogged with choking, blinding smoke. To add to the impression, yells and screams came from above and below the hanging miasma, and Ray nudged his partner on impatiently. This was no place to linger, and the two flattened their backs against the wall and side stepped up the stairs and around to the upper floor.

Pausing by the fire door to the third storey, Ray looked at Carl and raised three fingers in a countdown. Before he got to the final finger, The door erupted open and a big burly man in a black leather jacket spilled out into Carl's arms. They became entangled and, in a frenzy of confusion, started to wrestle right there on the landing. Ray could not intervene, as the doorway was busy with other men, equally distraught and vocal in their mania. Their attentions were held directly in front of them, at some convergence of horror that was far more pressing than the tower of hell behind Ray.

He raised his revolver, and stabbed out at them with it, yelling and snarling in the closest approximation of rage as his fear would allow. The men in the doorway were surprised by his emergence, and chose that time to flee, both from him and the terror they had been escaping. To see them on their way, Ray fired two rounds into the ceiling above them, the short barrel kicking up violently in his palm. The sound, in that enclosed corridor, was so immense to his unprotected ears, that Ray was instantly deafened but for a high pitched ringing that stung his ear drums. He lowered the gun with some disgust, while raising a hand to his stricken ears, but then noticed with dismay one of the fleeing gangsters had turned and raised his rifle. Ray ducked behind the stairwell entrance just in time, as a short spray of bullets whizzed down the corridor and splintered into the wood frame around him.

Snorting and grunting behind him revealed that Carl had managed to scramble up and get astride of the gang member on the landing, and was now slamming his head off of the floor. Ray was satisfied his partner had everything in hand and there was little he could do to assist. With few if any attractive options, Ray compelled himself to move on. The discovery of a viable exit and an end to this ordeal was paramount, so Knight sucked in three quick breaths and willed the adrenalin and hysteria to subside. Then, he re-entered the third floor corridor and began moving forward.

The smoke and debris were so thick, it was hard to make out anything with clarity. A body, twisted and charred beyond human recognition, lay to his right, and a pathetic figure crawled on its belly a metre from his foot, pulling itself slowly forward with clawing, clutching hands. Here, the red emergency lighting was offset by the blues and glitter of standing lamps and ambient atmospherics. No long stretch of doors and individual rooms on this floor; Shaun Meadows headquarters on this top storey were a lavish selection of large spaces, walls knocked through and wide, arched open doorways, allowing for the havoc to roam freely. Plush and expensive furnishing was overturned, or burned and smouldering with remnants of flame, while chairs and smashed glass were strewn everywhere the eye could see.

Toward the far end of the floor, facing the rear of the building, there was a perceptible eddy of fresh air stirring up the smoke into rolling, shifting shapes near the ceiling. As Ray advanced further, he made out a huge, jagged opening roughly in the centre of the rear wall, about fifteen feet wide, surrounded by rubble and masonry blown away from the gaping void. It was clear the damage was caused by an explosive force occurring from the outside directed inward, and explained the concussions they all heard earlier.

Ray pointed his revolver in front of him, squinting against the acrid gasses and murky coloured lighting. It took most of his remaining reserve to keep the barrel still, as he felt a trembling feeling grow within him, from his legs up and along his arms. Ahead of him, another room; impressively large, and from the glimpses of leather décor and gold trim, once quite grand. This had to be Shaun Meadows quarters, and what guards that had not fled already were lying lifeless in various poses of futile resistance, still clutching handguns, in all corners of the space.

A peculiar shape, black, upright and mobile, darted out of view. Ray swivelled and yelled out the familiar police force challenge. Against every jangling nerve in his body, he forced himself forward until he approached the doorway to Meadows' bedroom. The mysterious black figure there moved quickly and with thought, sweeping backward briefly to turn in his direction. Was it looking at him? Ray pointed the barrel of the snub nose toward this person, if that is what it was, and repeated his instruction to stop and drop. Instead, the dark shape began to rise and twist out of view, over the edge of one of the big panoramic windows. Ray yelled something while advancing hurriedly, and then felt the small gun kick backward again. He had squeezed the trigger, and by some sudden murderous impulse or release of built-up tension, two further massive bangs followed before the hammer clicked down on an empty chamber.

The glazing of the window was absent, and the smoke from within oozed out and trailed upward over the exterior of the building, as Ray gazed out. He lowered his pistol and rapidly took in three or four great lungfuls of oxygen and steadied himself by his other hand on the right of the sill. He noted the blue revolving lights of police response vehicles approaching, from under the Dunster bridge, and he knew there must be sirens as well, but he could not hear them, not with the constant ring in his ears. His head dropped, and that was when he noticed what looked for all the world like a big black spider, crouched at the lip of the frame. Squinting closer, he realised it was made of metal, a tool. A grappling hook, he suddenly realised.

That was not the strangest thing. A more disturbing image burned brighter in his mind right then and it refused to fade away. Of all the terrors he had endured and witnessed in that building, that last sight of the figure remained with him most doggedly. Unless in the chaos and horror he had quite lost all his senses and gone insane, he was certain that the figure he had seen looking back at him before leaping from the window, had been wearing some kind of long cloak. Either that, or he had wings.

13

Howard Watts was on the scene in person, so Ray guessed that either a phone call had been received from above, or the media attention had been so intense that he had been compelled to leave headquarters. Or both. Scanning the sky, several helicopters were sweeping low overhead, spots picking out clusters of officers trying to contain witnesses and the damage done to the third floor of the stricken building.

He could see them, but Ray could still barely hear them. The ringing from the gun discharges was still a constant annoyance, and no amount of swearing or rubbing at his ear would make it end. He guessed that most of the copters, about four or five he counted now, belonged to news channels, and around a hastily assembled perimeter, vans and camera crews were already jostling for prime position.

Ray was not surprised at the response, but still, the eye of the media brought nothing but added dread to the already dire circumstances. Now, there was a need to tread lightly and watch what they say, as well as try and clean up the shit storm where he had been placed, centre stage.

The armoured unit had rounded up many of the fleeing gang members, by now suitably recovered so they knew to discard their handguns and weapons; these now littered the road and curbs so this part of Blackbrook estate looked like the aftermath of some minor military campaign. The smoke and smouldering flames licking up the side of the third floor of the building also lent the whole atmosphere a scorched-earth effect, so the appearance of chaos and destruction was complete.

If Ray had had the energy left, he would have shook his head in wonder at the spectacle, but as it was, all he had the power to do right then was squat on the passenger seat of a patrol vehicle and try to control the trembling up and down his arms and legs.

The last thing he recalled doing in that cursed building, before the SWAT team had found them and he had been escorted to the exit in a storm of shouting, smoke and grasping hands, was entering Shaun Meadows' bed room. The scene stayed with him, despite all the helicopters and sirens, gunfire, panic and madness. There had been an odd stillness in that room; a disturbing quiet, made all the more unnerving by the bizarre placement of Shaun Meadow's body, on top of his wide, luxurious mattress. He looked almost serene, the large, tightly muscled forty-something, naked as a new born and doubled over, arms outstretched in a pliant, submissive pose of worship, beneath the large bloody smear decorating the wall before him. It was the killers calling card, an obscene figure in dark red, limbs splayed, and the wings unfurled as if to encompass and smother the sinner at its feet.

A stiff drink or a cigarette would have been welcome right then, but Ray knew he was about to get neither. When Howard noticed him, after several minutes of barking commands and directing the troops, he just regarded Ray with a barely contained snarl.

“You okay, Knight?” he asked, eventually. Ray looked at his boss and grimaced. For all of the terror and peril he had survived that evening, he observed that the gruff, steely appraisal of his superiors expression still had enough weight to inspire a little extra anxiety. “Meadows was not very talkative, Chief.” He tried his best to sound cocky, but the words came out in a sore croak, and prompted a bout of coughing that took Ray a moment to clear.

If Watts was concerned, he hid it well, and merely snorted at Ray’s remark. “Bring me the head of the fuck who did this, Raymond, and I’ll sign you off on indefinite paid leave, I promise.” With that, he left Ray where he was, with his head in his hands, and began bellowing and cursing at any officers who did not seem to be in an appropriate state of urgent activity.

Neat trousers and shoes approached the patrol vehicle and someone was leaning against the car door and calling Ray’s name. He looked up and registered an attractive young face, and more unusually, a look of genuine concern. He guessed it must have been one of the stations counsellors, despatched any time an officer reported coming under fire.

“Are you Raymond Knight?”

Ray nodded with zero enthusiasm, and answered the usual superficial questions that were regulation to ask. His face must have betrayed some kind of residual panic or shock, because the woman only appeared to become more phased.

“Really, detective, are you sure you wouldn’t want to come somewhere quiet and talk about this? Have the medics given you a proper check up yet?”

Despite his exhaustion, Ray was almost touched. He managed a smile, and with an almost vain, macho gesture, slowly and deliberately got to his feet and squared his shoulders. “I feel like shit, I won’t lie to you, but there’s plenty of dead guys in there who I suspect will be feeling a lot worse."

With that, the counsellor stiffened and most of the concern left her face. "Bravado, yes, that'll help. You know stress is one of the major killers among law enforcement? I'm serious."

Ray was about to reply that nine millimetre bullets were another major factor in shortening an officers career, and if she were to offer to compete all the paperwork he was facing after this fiasco, he would gratefully accept her help, but right then he noticed Carl Brooks emerging from the sweeping blue and red lightshow. He gestured with a finger and winked at the counsellor. "Now this guy, he might need your help."

When Carl saw Ray wave, he hopped gingerly over, clearly nursing some kind of sprain at his ankle, but with a wide beam over his face that Ray could only guess was dumb hysteria, that or he was genuinely surprised to see him still alive. They gripped each others shoulders, as much to maintain balance and assure each other they were still there, in the here and now.

Ray grinned at his partner, and when he spoke, he almost had to yell above the general din of sirens, shouts and engines. "Any holes where there shouldn't be any? You ready to pack in the job yet?"

Carl just shook his head. "Tonight was what I joined up for. Can we do it all again?" Ray momentarily doubted if his partner was telling a joke, then he straightened and took on a mock authoritative tone. "Don't get too excited, rookie, you're gonna have a shit load of paperwork to fill in after tonight, and I've delegated you in charge."

They both hunkered over instinctively as a helicopter swooped in low. In the background, they could still hear the bellows of Howard Watts trying to establish order. Ray aimed his voice in Carl's ear and pointed. "There's a lovely young lady over there," indicating the counsellor. "And she would love to talk about your feelings and emotions about tonight. One of the perks of the job. I advise a little restaurant somewhere, maybe candle light..."

Despite the noise and commotion, Carl still squinted in appraisal at the stern but attractive face, beside the patrol car. "I'm a happily married man, my wife wouldn't let me."

From a crowd of officers and raised voices behind them, another woman detached herself and made a bee line for the pair of detectives, abandoning a cameraman who was too encumbered to resist the restricting arms and clawing hands. She scampered before them, a heady rush of artfully arranged blonde curls and tantalising perfume, and thrust a microphone under their gawping chins.

"MBS news, Angela Draper – Were you the detectives on the scene?"

Those fixing, wide blue eyes caught Ray completely off guard, for about two seconds, before his training kicked in and he recognised the enemy

"Was notorious gangland kingpin Shaun Meadows among the murdered tonight, detective? Would you say this looks like a high level assassination?"

It was apparent that Ray was not the only one who had been temporarily bamboozled by the reporters manner, as he heard Carl beside him begin to mumble something in the affirmative. partially rejuvenated by the danger, Ray clasped his partners arm and spun him around, before glaring at the reporter with his most intimidating stare and growling a response, with firm finality.

"We have nothing to say at this stage."

Too late. Howard Watts had noticed, and roared with rage in their direction, while waving at some cowering officers trying to melt away beside him.

"What the fuck are those two still doing on the scene! I want them back at HQ for debrief in the next minute, or I'll have everyone's fucking badge. Lucas? What the living fuck is that reporter doing behind the barrier?"

Two escorting officers approached Ray and Carl and gestured without saying a word, but their insistence that they should repair to the patrol vehicle immediately was no less desperately implied. When Ray noticed the journalist named Draper begin to skip eagerly towards Watts, who had clearly betrayed himself as the man in charge, he decided this was indeed the most opportune time to be leaving the scene. He had no desire to see the fireworks that would ensue from that confrontation.

"Get us the fuck out of here, boys." he sang out, still pulling on Carl's arm. He briefly entertained the idea of feigning a mental breakdown and absconding with the counsellor; anything to avoid the toxic fall-out that was clearly coming to the boil, ever so nicely. *Could not have possibly gone any fucking worse*, thought Ray. *Not in my wildest fucking dreams*.

They left in a high whine of sirens and Blazing lights, but among the deafening and dazzling pandemonium that had overcome Blackbrook estate, their departure barely registered

14

Coffee, that miraculous heal-all. Ray nursed his mug between hands that were now mercifully under control, and the warmth and sweet taste (he had emptied two sachets of sugar into the cup, instead of the usual half) had temporarily made him forget how exhausted he was. He estimated that he had approximately one more hour in him until total collapse and mental shutdown. As it was, the chair he was sat in was a hard, cheap, plastic type, and he was not exactly being allowed to relax and enjoy the coffee in peace. Two gentlemen were very present with him in that small room, somewhere on the fourth floor of headquarters, and they ranged from placidly listening to him speak, to intently questioning his words.

If there was a name for these guys, whom Ray had probably met before and was told at the time, he thought it was something like 'public assurance', 'procedures governance', something along those lines. The people that initially check up on an incident that had gone public, to see if there may be any element that could make the department look bad, basically. Public Relations, or *pen-pushing PR pricks*, as Ray labelled them.

It looked like any and every office, except in this one, there were no windows, bar the one in the door, and Ray was tempted to request to smoke a cigarette, just to annoy the two suits studying him very carefully. His request would have been casually refused, and moreover, to provoke these guys in any way would be a declaration of psychological warfare, a war he was in no shape to wage.

"And how certain are you, would you say, that the eruptions occurred prior to any gunfire? Might Carl Brooks see it any differently, do you think?" This from the man seated directly opposite Ray, who said everything over a pair of thick black spectacles, while making a show of running a pencil down a notepad in front of him. His demeanour was not exactly unpleasant or threatening, more like appealingly neutral, which was no doubt the demeanour they had both come to perfect for the job.

Ray remembered at least, from experience and from countless peer-advisory warnings, to keep his responses as brief and non-descriptive as possible. He only wished he had had the foresight to pre-warn Carl to do likewise. *The big jerk is probably giving them his fucking life story,* he thought, so loudly that he was sure that they both would hear. Instead, he cleared his throat and forced out "I'm sure Carl would recollect events in the same way I have described them."

The man nodded enthusiastically, apparently appeased by that, while at the same time crossing out something on the note paper. Hopefully a surplus item on a grocery list, thought Ray, as he glanced for the umpteenth time at thc clock above the door to gauge how long he had been in this room. He noticed, through the doorway, that a big screen television was on in the main room out there, kept tuned to a news channel that much of the immediate staff were taking a keen interest in. Heads looked up to the screen, engrossed, and Ray was eager to gauge for himself what merry story the media had weaved around that nights fun and games. The second man beside the shelving in the corner, who seemingly was there to keep an eye on the man whose job it was to keep an eye on people, spoke up for the first time.

"Did your partner discharge his weapon at any time this evening, do you recall?"

Ray drained the last of the coffee in his mug and drew in a long breath to brace himself. We're at the meat and potatoes of our little chat. He tried to keep his gaze level and steady as he replied, in the negative.

"And did you discharge your weapon at any time, detective?"

Ray swallowed, and prolonged the opportunity to collect his thoughts by retrieving a toothpick from his jacket pocket and bringing it to his mouth, to gnaw on anxiously. Despite only just finishing his mug of coffee, his throat felt suddenly very dry and raw, so, after a minute, he simply nodded and hummed in the affirmative. A slight raise in the eyebrow, perhaps indicating the man's interest peaking at that moment, or else he was getting excited at the prospect of catching his man out. *Sadistic little preening jobsworth.*

As if he had heard Ray, the man opened his hands and raised his tone to sounds sympathetic and agreeable. "I can assure you I'm only asking this for purposes of due process, and I fully understand you may be in no condition to recall exactly what occurred, exactly as it happened, I'm just asking you to volunteer information that the department may find useful, or that we can work with to move this case on. I don't want to take up any more of your time than I have to, detective Knight, and want to see you home with as much compassionate leave as you feel necessary."

He's playing the friend card with me, he knows this is make or break time.

"Did you have an individual as target at the time you opened fire, do you recall? Are you able to recall if you hit your target?"

Ray's shoulders sank and his eyes dropped to the floor, The image of the figure at the window, the one with wings, vividly came back to him, amid the smoke and red haze. He suddenly felt all the adrenalin that he had been feeding off escape him, to be replaced by pain, tiredness and anxious doubt. The hour he had guessed at had been reduced to ten minutes with the asking of that question, and Ray frowned deeply as the toothpick worked busily in his mouth.

"I . . .I think I hit him, yes. I mean, my aim was true enough, I thought . . . I was sure at the time..."

More eager nods of encouragement. "Go on, detective. What happened?"

Ray sighed, and no matter how much he willed himself to, he could not look up to meet those black spectacles, and the busy, searching eyes behind them. "Nothing." he said, quietly.

"I'm sorry, did you say nothing happened? How many times did you open fire exactly? You did say you thought you were on target, correct?"

Ray's eyes remained firmly fixed on the scuff marks around the top of his shoes. "yes," he said, more positively this time, and louder. "I shot the suspect; Twice, I believe. But it had no effect."

15

Filthy, rusty-coloured water stained the sides of the bathtub which was giving off a reek of anti-sceptic. Still dripping, the man dabbed his body dry in a long mirror, and then opened the big zip-lock plastic bag of bandages and medication. The codeine dulled his pain receptors but it was the diazepam which was currently calming his nerve endings and allowing him to focus more leisurely on the task at hand. He grasped the beaker of fruit and vegetable smoothie, drained it in several long, slow pulls, then raised a shaving mirror to examine parts of himself in detail.

There was some massive bruising on his calves and thighs, and a deep graze had very nearly opened up a major artery. The bruising continued over his hips and reached his ribs, where a tentative prod confirmed several were likely cracked. At his shoulder, a bullet had gouged out an ugly trough of flesh, which would clearly need treating first. He selected the appropriate applications and began to carefully wrap, seal and patch as thoroughly as anyone could have.

An hour later, dressed in thick thermals, the man sat at the bench and consumed a protein rich meal he had prepared himself, and then reclined on a high leather settee and commenced the meditation he had learned and practised to best promote healing. He had already spent the time in his bath reviewing and observing the media coverage from the completed mission, hopping from channel to channel, and felt assured that it had gone as well as he could have expected. Sleep, and more importantly rest, would be deep and satisfying.

Tomorrow, he would begin the hot and cold treatments, alternately steaming, sweating and freezing, while tending to the repairs to the armour and his suit. The chest plate was dented and scratched in numerous places, and the layers of polycarbon feathers would need reinforcing. More medical applications, many more supplements and steroids, and by the evening, he could recommence some basic exercises and strength training. By the following day, he would expect to be ready for the weights and bars, and more importantly, some patrol and reconnaissance. There was no time to lose. Society's imagination had a wickedly short time limit, and what he had started yesterday may be forgotten the following week. This momentum was too precious to lose, and it was vital to sustain.

And besides, the bad in the world never rested, and never retreated.

He had identified the next target and was certain it would send the right message. This one was less fixed and less predictable, more tricky to pin down. He had to move quickly while his data was still fresh and reliable, but not compromise on strategy and preparation. In this case, the mind must move faster than the hand.

Shaun Meadows was a crude and brazen criminal, who gloried in his notoriety, but this one, the one that he had singled out, was far more secretive and cunning. His glories were less touted, and his crimes were well hidden. Meadows was used to and habituated to violence, and he was delivered to an appropriate end. But this new target, he removed himself from the dirty work and instead languished in a bubble of privilege and luxury. It was going to be a pleasure to burst that bubble, and break the man within.

*

Ray was aware that the best way to get to sleep and rest was to try not to. Television was out of the question; after a minute or two of switching channels, it was clear there was only one incident hogging the headlines that evening, and there was a real danger he might happen to see himself on the screen, getting ambushed by that Angela Draper witch.

It was common after extraordinary events, like the one he had just come through, to be offered a period of compassionate leave; often to privately assess accountability and liability to the department as much as to limit any trauma the officer may have suffered. Ninety nine times out of a hundred, Raymond Knight would have readily accepted, leapt at the opportunity in fact, and credit to Watts, his boss had given him the option, albeit in a resentful growl that made it clear he would prefer Ray to man it out and stick around.

Ray may have expected some recognition for getting himself and a rookie out of that slaughterhouse, which he had objected to visiting in the first place, but it was not brownie points that he was interested in scoring. His life had been seriously endangered, and he wanted nothing more then to find out why, and how he could prevent it happening again. The scowl on his Captain's face had momentarily lifted when he had said he would be back in the morning, looking almost as surprised as Ray felt in hearing him say those words. But still, he appreciated the silent nod Watts gave him, which served as the only kind of praise he was ever likely to get from the senior man.

Shortly after returning to his apartment that night, however, Ray had begun to doubt if he had done the wise thing. His knees had barely lasted till he got to his front door, and the old tear in the tissue of his left shoulder had flared up again at some point during his exertions; the whole arm was now stiff with a throbbing pain, as he had discovered when he tried to remove his jacket and shirt.

After consuming half a cold pizza he found in the fridge, and a very long, very hot shower, Ray had stretched out on his settee, in his training sweater and pants, with little energy to do anything else but lie there and breathe. For the first time in a long while, he felt something approaching safety, lying there in the dark, listening to the busy sounds of the city come to him, from far away, and watch the pattern of traffic lights moving slowly across his wall.

Snippets of sound and images from earlier raced through his mind. Yells of fear and bloody twisted faces combined with the roar of gunfire. Unlike his body, the signal to his brain to shut off was clearly not getting through. If he had had a packet of cigarettes or tobacco to hand, he was certain that he would be smoking furiously by now, and probably, to his disgust, would be enjoying doing so. A toothpick would be no consolation. In the end, Ray resorted to reverse psychology; if his mind was consumed with the terrors of recent events, then he would not resist it, and he started to recap what had gone wrong, and when.

First it had been the pusher, in the dark alley,

which led to Meadows, a criminal overlord, all courtesy of this maniac with wings. But Darlow; Why him? He was in his apartment, never to have been found if it had not been for a nosey neighbour and a noisy dog. His body had been discovered, it had not been found in public and on display. To Ray's mind, his killing did not quite fit with the others, and the connection to the department and himself was all too troubling.

Darlow had only recently been released, but that was not exactly common knowledge, and his crimes were not exactly recent memory. There was history there, but what about the relevance?

Ray mustered up the strength to prepare a big mug of hot chocolate before he settled himself once more on the sofa and pulled his laptop over onto his knees. He stared down at the screen with the help of some reading glasses.

Entry into the police systems was discouraged and complicated after work hours, but it could be done, with use of the correct passwords and procedures that Ray had been taught. He was less certain of the correct software and records that he had to access to get the information that he thought he needed.

Archives turned up the case file on Richard Darlow, and from there, he was able to bring up the victim profiles. Nearly an hour had passed by the time he arrived at the correct data, and as a stream of names, links and report logs began to scroll past Ray's eyes, he was already nodding off to sleep.

16

When the news anchor spoke, hs voice was carefully inflected with concern, although the flawless complexion of his face hardly changed. “Angela, Have you been able to find out the cause of last night's carnage? Are we talking gangland retaliation, terrorists or...what?”

The screen behind the anchor changed to frame the face of an attractive young woman, blonde, and discretely made over to accentuate her best features. “Yes, as we all learned yesterday, this was the domain of the notorious gang leader Shaun Meadows, which he used as headquarters from which to carry out his many criminal activities. His brother Trent, currently serving a twelve year sentence, had mastered similar vices; Drugs, arms dealing and extortion, to list but a few, so it was only natural to assume that what happened yesterday was some kind of brutal grab for power or shift in the power structure of this city’s criminal underworld. The damage and violence that took place, of which we can only observe the aftermath, I understand has been apparently quite professional and even sophisticated. I think it is fair to say that this was no random attack or rival exchange of gun fire. This was a major operation.”

The news anchor’s face changed slightly with the addition of a small frown. “Are you saying this may not be gang related, Angela? Could this be an operation by our governments secret services, or another countries, possibly?”

The woman's voice had been clear and precise so far in the broadcast, but now her tone took on a higher, more urgent and eager element. "that I can't tell you for certain, Brian, but I am able to tell you that MBS News has an exclusive for you this morning, as we have secured a witness who is willing to talk to us about the event yesterday. Craig Maitland was actually in the building at the time of the attack and joins me now," The camera zoomed out from the reporter to reveal the man stood beside her. He was late twenties, early thirties in age, with a baseball cap on and stood quite awkwardly, with his eyes flicking from the camera lens to the woman and back again. He was clearly not used to being on camera and his body language confirmed it.

"Craig, you knew Shaun Meadows, didn't you? You were, effectively, a member of his gang, would that be fair to say?"

The anxiety level of the young man increased noticeably and an uncomfortable smirk came to his face. "I used to do some work for Shaun, yeah, you could say that, but I wouldn't call myself a gangster, if that's what you're saying. I was brought up around here, this is a poor area," The looks into the camera intensified, as the man seemed to try and plead some imaginary case. "Many of the kids around here took up work for Shaun and his brother at one time or another. After Trent Meadows got locked up then it was just Shaun who was the big man around the block. We looked up to him. And it was regular, steady money. That ain't so easy to come by, in this part of the city."

The woman tried to placate the man by placing a hand on his arm, and softening her voice an octave. "I understand, Craig, and I'm sure our viewers sympathise, but can you confirm that you were actually in the building behind us at the time of the attack yesterday, and perhaps shed some light into what actually happened for our viewers?"

At this the man brightened, as if he had identified a quick means to elevate his status. "Oh yeah, I was there, Ms Draper, I was right on the third floor when that psycho came in. I heard all the explosions and bullets and sh...stuff; I was right there."

"You used the word 'psycho', are you saying that it was one individual that did all this we can see now? How could that be possible?"

The man was all wide, beaming smiles now, and he shifted from one foot to the other in excitement. "Yeah, I wasn't in the room with Shaun directly, you understand, but I was there hanging out with some friends of mine when - BLAM! The whole damn wall comes crashing in and the noise of the explosion just freaks us all out, you know? We all thought the world had come to an end, or it was nuclear war or an earthquake or something, but then, we all started getting our senses back and the smoke kinda cleared and we could see this wasn't no natural disaster or anything like that,"

The woman interrupted him, more to stem his rapidly uncontrolled babbling than for clarification. "You said it was an individual, one, no more than two men – a 'psycho' - that attacked you that day. Can you explain more about that and perhaps tell us who you thought this person was?"

"Shoot, I never seen this dude before, not in normal like reality life. He just comes flying in and throwing bombs around and grenades and stuff like that, and it was so fast, some of the guys there, the ones close to Shaun, barely had time to get their guns out or pull the trigger. This guy was so quick, racing around everywhere, it was like impossible to get a sight on him, man, you know what I mean? And anyone that did manage to get a round off, they were like blown up or taken out, you know what I'm saying? It was crazy, just crazy."

"And you say it was one man? Did you get a look at him?"

"Well, it was hard to see, you know? With the smoke and everything, and everyone was scared and running around and stuff. It was the kind of situation you do NOT want to participate in, you know what I'm saying? I just wanted to get the hell out of there as fast as I could, I can't lie to you, but yeah, I got a look at the guy. Shoot, there was no forgetting this dude once you seen him, he was one wacky-looking son of a you-know-what, you know what I'm saying? The guy had on some kind of suit, you know, like with armour and stuff, so when you shot at him, the bullet just pinged off, you know? He'd just keep on coming. And the wacky headgear he was sporting and the wings..."

The camera zoomed in and the microphone rose closer to the man's mouth, while the reporter's tone became more urgent. "Sorry, did you say 'wings'? This man had on some kind of special suit and had...what else?"

The smile faded slightly as a self-conscious doubt abruptly doused the gang members enthusiasm. He glanced nervously down at the microphone and then back up at the camera. "Yeah, you know, feathers and stuff? Wings. Not real birds wings, I guess, some kind of reinforced or armour plated shit, excuse my language. The helmet was some kind of metal, too, you know? This guy was ready, you know what I'm saying? He had come prepared. He had not just showed up to discuss the weather or chill and watch some TV or nothing like that. He meant business."

The camera panned over to frame the reporters face once more, which now glowed with a kind of satisfaction that only showed itself in the sparkles of her wide blue eyes. "Well there you have it, Brian. Genuine testimony from a cohort of Shaun Meadows, at ground zero, as it were. And if we thought we were going to get any answers today, I think we can all agree that our whole thinking on the event yesterday has just taken a turn for the bizarre, and this story only has more questions and mysteries to come."

Howard Watts pushed the button on his zapper and the television blinked off. He leant back in his chair, his eyes still looking toward the screen but unfocussing far into the distance, as he let out a long and protracted sigh. With grim trepidation, his eyes dropped to the telephone on his desk, and he waited for it to ring. He did not wait long.

17

Carl Brooks felt pretty good. The job had exceeded his expectations so far, and even if the things he had heard about his new partner were true, at least he was not dull. He nodded and smiled at everyone he saw on the department floor that morning, and before he even reached his desk, the

Captain, cradling a telephone between his chin and his shoulder, snapped his fingers for his attention and waved him toward interview room one, which in fact was the Chief's own meeting room, when he had big-wigs over. Carl pushed open the door, and was greeted with a curt nod by Tom Jameson and about a dozen other officers, some of them looking like they had skipped sleep that night.

"Hey Brooks, how you feelin'?" the question seemed genuine enough, but from the intense scrutiny of Jameson's eyes, scanning him up and down, Carl knew this was also a crash suitability assessment. "I'm just dandy," he replied, in a loud, clear voice, making the most of his height and size, so he almost looked down at the head of operations. "Happy to be on board!"

Jameson's eyes lingered a moment more, and then with a nod, seemed to perform a mental tick against Carl's name, and turned to regard the men behind him. "This is Peters and Jacobs," gesturing to the tired looking guys, both unshaven and shirts loose at the necks. "They're profile and Eval. This is Williams and Lalonde, Balistics and Tactical," a solid, imposing couple of men. If they had missed any sleep in the last week, they would not have shown it. "And we got some forensics here, duty officers, as well as Mr Richardson there from the secretary's office." He was government, Carl guessed. The stakes were clearly high as many eyes were apparently watching. He chose not to relax himself on one of the upholstered chairs, and instead reposed against one of the many tables, looking ready and attentive. Jameson stopped beside a double-size presentation stand, where there were numerous interesting graphics, photographs and big, capitalized words adjoining arrows pointing to different documents. Carl recognised the images of the wingman, with three photographs lined along the bottom of the stand.

"You seen Knight?" Jameson asked him suddenly, catching Carl off guard. "Uh, no, Gov, I came straight up from the garage. Maybe he's stuck in traffic?" A harrumph from Jameson and a scowl was all his reply earned, and Carl was happy for the subject to trail off in a hot funk. There was clearly lots of work to be updated on, and yet to do, so Carl waited for the debriefing to commence in earnest.

"Officers Noble and Irving interviewed the witnesses at length and individually, until release this morning. All six of them provided corroboration of roughly the timescale of events and the suspect we are focussed on. Carl, you confirmed you got to building A at about six that evening, and by your guess, you think the first concussion occurred about half an hour later. We're still awaiting returns on data from the CCTV in the area, prior to that time, to see if we pick up our suspect anywhere in the city, on the approach. Dave, you have an idea what the hardware may have been that was used to force entry?"

The one identified as Lalonde leant forward. "Yeah, it was likely miniature detonators, similar to the old limpet mines we use on subs and tankers," He glanced toward the forensics crew, who seemed to nod in affirmation. "Military grade, effective in clearing the masonry to the extent we can see at the scene. It would have taken out the windows at the same time, more than sufficient to gain entry"

His partner, Williams, cleared his throat and leant forward then. "I'm confident he was concealed in this area," He gestured to a complicated, diagramatic map of what Carl assumed had to be the corner of Blackbrook estate. "From the adjacent roof, he could have rapelled to an area a safe distance away, triggered the detonation, then rapelled the rest of the way and swung in through the opening."

Jameson interjected. "Again, we're hoping CCTV can affirm these details for us. What's your opinion on the armoury, given the witnesses testimony?"

Williams continued. "I think its safe to say there was some kind of kevlar based body suit at the base, secured with steel chest plates and reinforced boots. The face visor likely some kind of strengthened fibreglass resin, and the wings likewise, a composite of thin, protected carbon plates. Lightweight, manoeuvrable and with good levels of protection. Overall, I'm not surprised he resisted the handgun or semi automatic rounds for as long as he did, but they would still have packed a punch. That's why I'm thinking there was some kind of adrenal booster supplement involved. To take the abuse he did and keep moving, takes a bit more than willpower alone."

Jameson indicated a graphic that Carl had noticed early on and stood out from all the rest on the busy board. It was a detailed mock up of what the tactics man had just described, combined, he guessed, with what the witnesses had seen. The picture showed an impressive and intimidating figure, not unlike some character from some of the Saturday morning cartoons he used to watch as a kid, or from the movies that were always popular in the cinema chains at the moment. 'Superhero', is the word that came to mind.

"Larry, can you give us any insight on what kind of guy we could be dealing with here?" Jameson was talking to the man he had identified earlier as Peters, the psychological evaluation specialist. He hastily put down the mug of hot brew he was drinking from and cleared his throat. "Loner, or living with parents. No more than middle aged, probably younger. He's experienced some kind of history of oppression or has heightened sensitivity to inferiority. Probably experienced some kind of episode of radical imposition, a jump, if you like, from the real to the imaginary, or hyper-real. Now, I would guess..."

Right then, everyone's attention was diverted toward the door, as Howard Watts entered the room. Carl was half hoping it might be Ray, but now that the Chief was present, Carl thought a late entry by Raymond would probably prove more negative than if he missed this meeting entirely. Howard wasted no time in making his wishes felt, and hesitated only to nod in the direction of the government man, Richardson (Carl could see where his anxieties lay, from that gesture).

"Morning men, I know we've been working overtime already on this case, but I hope by now you realise the urgency of this one and the need to close it down as soon as we all possibly can," Watts looked as exhausted as anyone in the room, and with his shirt cuffs rolled up and two days growth on his chin, looking generally a mess, Carl realised that cases like this must not be that common place, and he was embroiled in something pretty unusual. "Nothing can stir up public feeling or feed headlines faster than a vigilante, particularly a successful one," Watts glanced behind him to the picture on the stand. "And we need to find and stop this one before the public get wind of his 'Superman' delusion."

Carl's eyes glazed over then, as he listened to the Captain. He wondered at the idea of the 'superhero', and recalled the films he had watched in the past. The thought of someone dressed in a suit, heavily armed and with clear psychological issues, harming and killing people in the city, was something that should not be at all attractive to a sane person. But then, the news stations seemed to be occupied with nothing else, and everyone he passed on his way to work had been talking about it. When the Captain asked a question, he snapped out of his reverie and raised his hand.

"Yes, Brooks?"

"Yeah, I was gonna say, given the threat this guy seems to present, shouldn't we be issued with, I dunno, some firepower that packs a little more punch. I mean, a single pistol doesn't look like its gonna get the job done." He instantly noticed a few of those gathered exchange some meaningful looks, after he had finished, and Carl reddened with indignation.

"Noted, Carl." Howard's reply came after a beat. "Tactics will fill us in on that score shortly, but for now, I called this meeting to show how important it is we all work together. If we utilize all our talents to the full and put in a good shift, I see no reason why we can't get a result in the next few days. And it does need to be that fast gentlemen, am I right?" This to the Eval guys, Peters and Jacobs, who nodded in turn. "We can't afford for any one of us to slack off or not put in their bit."

The door opened, and Carl's heart sank. The chief looked round, as did everyone in the room right then, as Raymond Knight stood at the doorway looking lost.

18

For once, Ray was relieved to get to his desk. He did not resent the mirthful poking his partner subjected him to. The grin Brooks wore right then was the healthy sign of someone not taking everything too seriously, and he was a world away from the self righteous asshole that was now the acting head of ops, Jameson.

"Shit, dude, you ever seen the right side of Watts, or you pride yourself on being the biggest thorn in his side?" Carl wasted no time in logging in to the system, and since yesterday, the only thing Ray observed that had been added to his desk was a protein shaker and some candy wrappers. "Is this some kind of ploy for early retirement?"

Ray glared at him and grunted. "You should thank me, rookie, deflecting the amateurish mistakes of your sorry ass"

Carl's grin widened. "Why were you late anyway, I can't picture you a big sleeper."

Ray stabbed at the keys of his computer, in the accustomed sequence, to entice it to life. He had no idea what he was going to do once he logged in.

"You're right, your sleep is the first to go on this job. Then your sex drive," He said this with emphasis, and watched with some satisfaction some of the mirth drain from his partners face. "But, to be honest with you, I was thinking about the case, which is not something I ever recommend anyone do when you're not here and on your own time."

Jameson and Watts had allocated Ray and Carl to review the Darlow case, due to Ray's first hand insight into it, and try dig up any cohorts or possibly overlooked characters from the files. As a casual affront to Ray, before he left the meeting, Watts advised Carl directly to "...keep Ray out from under everyone's feet." Much to Carl's amusement, but the comment was far less cutting than the one that Jameson had dealt him, while handing him the summary file. "You think you can handle that, Knight?" using his last name like that, and with a dead cold expression of contempt all over his face. *'How about an uppercut to that narrow jaw of yours?'* Ray had thought. *'Could you handle that?'* and he had visualised the prime locations around the man's body which he considered looked vulnerable to a stout jab or knuckle thrust. Physically assaulting the Head of Operations in front of his colleagues would certainly put paid to his law enforcement career, no matter how efficiently he went about it.

The rigours of the morning were not over after the meeting, as both himself and Carl were then instructed to attend the 'compulsory press training' brief with the relations team. This entailed an hour plus of example video footage and discussions and quizzes, much of which Ray had gone through previously. He understood that every sensitive case like this had to involve some kind of training of this nature. It was essential every officer now had to understand how to respond to closed questions that require a 'yes' or a 'no' – by answering with anything BUT a 'yes' or a 'no' - and how to respond to open ended questions – having set phrases prepared and memorised. He found it pretty tedious, but nonetheless kept glancing at Carl to make sure he was taking all of it in. If that attractive blonde reporter for MBS started batting her eyelashes at the young man again, he hoped Carl would be better able to deal with it next time.

They were not dismissed until lunch time, and by then, the pair of them were relieved to mix with the rest of the squad and return to normality. What Ray really did appreciate and was grateful for, was the re-allocation of much of his current cases, and the paperwork that came with them. So, gone was the messy domestic shooting over on East side, and likewise the double overdose on Hathaway and the floater that washed up on the banks of the Dunster last Tuesday. He would not miss them at all, and hoped he would not discover which of his lucky colleagues had ended up with them on their desk.

Regardless, even with the freeing up of his time, the last thing Knight wanted to do right then was read page after page of case notes, ten years old, from a time in his life he had tried very hard to forget. His eyes focussed on nothing, as he scrolled up and down his email inbox page, and when Carl asked him how far back he thought they should look into the file archive, Ray just shrugged.

"I guess if you solved the case and dragged our wingman in to Watts' office, hog-tied and gagged, that might win you back some favour and grace," Carl offered, before turning to look closer at his distracted partner. "Why? What did you find out at home, you sly old goat?"

Ray turned to regard the younger man and lowered his voice to speak confidentially. "Look, lets forget all this shit for now and take a moment or two to think about this. We're not going to get to the bottom of this tapping on keyboards. Darlow is the key here. The other guys, I can understand, street dogs and gangsters, great, the world may well be a better place without them."

Carl's grin vanished as he considered the senior

man's words. "But Darlow, he was on nobodies shit list," He spoke as he thought. "A paedophile, yes, but how would our man know that?"

Ray nodded. "Exactly, that shit looked personal, I'd bet my pay on it."

When Carl suggested they open the file and take a closer look, Ray told him not to bother, and produced a crumpled list from one of his jacket pockets.

"Tell me you got the name of the Wingman on that paper."

Ray grimaced. "No, listen. There were about a dozen parents that lost a child to that sick fuck-ball, but I checked them all out. We got a profile of our suspect now, haven't we? Turns out, several of those kids had no father that they knew about, some others are now too old to fit the profile or are dead. I got this list down to only two couples, living in the city limits."

Carl frowned. "So, you're thinking … " Ray could not wait for his partner to finish the thought, so gave him a helpful prompt. "Think about it. What would you do, if your precious little boy was abused and murdered, and you knew the fuck who done it?"

Carl met the older man's eyes and he saw the promise there that was beginning to dawn in his own mind. "A man, probably in his forties, aggrieved..." he began to recite from the summary folder on his desk. Ray nodded encouragement, and they both fell into a contemplative silence.

"You got addresses?"

19

Good old fashioned legwork. The act of actually knocking on doors, talking to people, taking statements. It made up a good proportion of many officers duties, and it reminded Ray of his earlier days on patrol, before he became a detective. They used Ray's old Toyota so they would not have to sign off on the form for a patrol vehicle, but Carl still drove as Ray was using the time in the passenger seat to try and remember the victim profiles and his visits to the relatives nearly ten years previous. It seemed like yesterday.

The closest address was out by Marine Walk, which was an expanding collection of two story semis near to the river mouth. Lucas Roszinsky was twelve when he had been abducted and murdered, and the file photo showed a bashful looking kid in shorts, still too skinny for the height he was clearly growing into. Ray recalled that the parents had been hard to contact because of the heavy work schedule they both maintained, and when he had broke the news to them, it was the father who had crumbled and the mother who had stayed upright and stoic. She had questioned him thoroughly on the suspect and his predictions on the outcome of the trial.

As they approached the suburb, his partner noticed how silent he became, and when Carl glanced over, Ray was looking thoughtfully out of the window, looking every bit his fifty three years of age. A toothpick flicked around his lips as he chewed on it thoughtfully, trying to think of the things to say when he met with Mr and Mrs Roszinsky again. Would they remember him? Would they resent him being there, feeling betrayed and let down by what the department had done? And then, the sting of grief and despair, from a couple that have had their child cruelly robbed from them; would that still be present, in the air? Ray imagined what it might be like to lose his Catherine, and how ten years might make any difference to the rage and sorrow that would have consumed him.

Carl pulled up on the road outside a brick dwelling much like all the others in that suburb, and Ray remembered how before, it had looked very neat and new, whereas now, this house more than the others looked a little shabby and neglected. The soffits and facias around the roof looked a little warped, and the small front lawn was noticeably overgrown and strewn with litter. Ray gestured for Carl to wait, while he got out and walked slowly up to the front door.

Mrs Roszinsky answered on the second knock, and regarded the detective with no sign of recognition. She made no move to invite Ray inside when he greeted her and explained who he was, and instead he stood in her doorway and looked furtively over her shoulder.

"Is your other half in at all, Mrs Roszinsky?"

Her eyes narrowed. "Why you wish to know?"

Ray blustered through his hastily prepared explanation, how he was from a victim support initiative, and was going through some of his old cases, checking up and seeing if they could help in any way. Mrs Roszinsky just looked him up and down with something like astonishment, as if she could not comprehend how he had come to be on her doorstep. Her jaw worked to articulate this surprise, but before she could actually get any words out, an abrupt and shrill bark came from behind her.

"Who is it, Rosa?"

The woman looked over her shoulder to where the voice had come from, then back to the detective on her doorstep. Ray stood fast against this frosty reception, and tried to press forward during her momentary hesitation. "We have on our files that Mr Roszinsky was working for Bishops pharmacists, is that still correct?"

"John hasn't worked for three years, officer. Not in his condition."

It was Ray's turn to struggle for words, but as if to clarify, Mrs Roszinsky seemed to make a decision and opened the door wider, retreating in to the hallway and clearly inviting Ray to follow. He joined her and saw beyond into a living room, with a single plush armchair near the door and a middle aged gentleman sat there facing forward. His hands gripped tightly to the chairs arms and his gaze never left the middle distance. His hair was prematurely whitened, so that he looked older than the figure Ray had calculated Mr Roszinsky must be.

"I look after him now, ever since the breakdown. We get little support but, you know… it does not go far, and I cannot work so many hours at the agents"

Ray noticed now her deeply lined features and the harried knit to her brow. He had seen relationships sour and crumble after the death of a child before, and it was always heartbreaking. This couple had obviously never recovered from the loss of Lucas and this weight had taken a far more destructive toll on them than the case ever had on Ray. He took a long breath and shut his eyes for a moment, and then he apologised for disturbing them both and politely excused himself.

When he returned to the Toyota, Carl could see at

once his mood had taken an even more sombre plunge. Ray took his seat without even glancing at Carl, and only growled out of the side of his mouth the one word; "Drive." and Carl silently obeyed. Once they were back on the highway, he braved a question, but had to wait for the answer. Ray was staring out of the passenger window again, brooding, and did not look around when he replied. "It's not Mr Roszinsky."

Carl drove in silence a minute more. "You're pretty sure about that?"

"It's not him. The man is... he's not well."

Carl hesitated before continuing. "The profile says our wingman would have experienced major mental disruption in the last three years. It's not for us to say what a disturbed mind may be capable of, we aren't psyche and eval." He glanced over to gauge the reaction of his words, and noted the big man's uncomfortable flex at his shoulder. He was considering it, but Carl was not about to push the point.

"Just get to the Lowe family," Was all that Ray eventually said.

Carl slowed the Toyota a quarter of an hour later outside a small estate on one of the more affluent areas of the city's West side. Tall, sturdy iron gates enclosed the buildings, which were all modern, three storey blocks, with an apartment occupying each floor. Carl had to show his badge at a security monitor for the gates to swing inward and allow them to enter and pull up in the small lot outside block four. Wide expanses of lawn separated each building, and numerous colourful play areas were well placed about the grounds, busy with the laughter and squeals of young children, enjoying their time in the rare mid afternoon sun. The whole area was an altogether jollier place that did exactly what it was designed to do; provide a safe and comfortable enclave from the crime and pollution of the inner city.

The pair found the intercom for Block four, and buzzed at the number for the apartment listed as the residence of Mr and Mrs Lowe. The tinny voice at the speaker asked them to confirm their identity and business, and after a short pause, the buzzer rang out for Ray to push open the lobby doors. They hopped up the stairwell to floor two, and knocked their arrival at the front door there. Within a second or two, the door was opened by a woman in her mid forties, at most, with long straight auburn hair and wearing a knitted sweater and jeans. She had an attractive appearance, but the crows feet at her eyes were noticeable, and Ray recalled speaking to a much younger looking mother at the time of the conviction. As much as he tried, he could not recall the face of the husband, or even what he might have said when they talked together.

Mrs Lowe fixed them both with piercing grey eyes, which matched the shrewdness in her demeanour as she put to them plainly and directly that 'They were here about Dominic.' Ray swallowed and remarked that yes, they were here about her son, and at once dismissed the idea of persisting with any cover story he had concocted. She looked them up and down a moment more, and then stepped back so they could to enter. Carl spoke up then.

"Thank you Mrs Lowe. Would Mr Lowe be able to join us?"

"No he will not," She answered matter of factly. "I do not know where my husband is."

20

The information had been seeded, and would decrypt itself the moment the user clicked on the link at the bottom of his message. Information was a precious commodity, and its control and manipulation was part of the arsenal of his enemies. The Devil hid himself in the details, and maybe now, he thought, people would seek out information and use it as the potential weapon it could be. Shine a light on these monsters, and they were sure to scurry in fright back to the darkness.

He had included his motif, and his name, and relished the rise in stakes that his deed would elicit, and all from the confines of his computer screen. Perhaps all of his objectives could have been achieved via the world wide web? What a thought. As if to expel it from his mind, he raised from his chair and crossed to the armoury cabinet, reaching for the moulded chest plate and securing it about his torso. He lifted the twin appendages and lowered them over his shoulders, the weight of them forcing his back upright. And then, finally, the helmet, which slid over his face and seemed to transform him truly into being complete again.

Removing a moulded steel dart from his belt, he twisted swiftly from the hips and released it from the flick of his wrist, embedding the tip deep into the timber of a cross beam. He felt strong, and decided then it was time to go on patrol, roam among the masses and hunt down and corner one of the lower forms. Remove them from the population and practice some of his talents.

*

Her apartment was spacious and well decorated. Despite some toys and children's clothes, strewn here and there, it was clear the place was meticulously and thoughtfully maintained, as a devoted mother would do. There was the clear presence of a child that made the place a home, and from the look of the belongings and framed snaps on the sideboards and walls, it was a young girl, Ray guessed. He perched on the far seat of a sofa and Carl settled into the matching chair beside it. Mrs Lowe stood looking at them with her arms crossed in front of her chest, leaning against the island unit of the kitchen area. It was clear she was not about to offer them a cup of coffee.

Her voice was stern and defiant when she spoke. "What is it that you want?"

Ray remembered the baby crying from the room next door, when he was here last, trying and failing to console the couple. That child must be all grown up now, it was that long ago. He remembered her face, creasing and trembling as she lost control, and he could remember her husband, being sat next to her. But that was it; he could not recall what he had said or much of how he had reacted. He just seemed to go very quiet. As he ransacked his memory, Carl was trying to mumble something polite about intruding and not taking up too much of her time, and Ray could see what little patience she may have had for their being there was already reaching its limit.

"We need your help." Ray said, plainly and clearly, over the voice of his partner. Mrs Lowe moved her gaze and fixed him with it. He could see the history of hurt in her eyes, as they tried to read his face.

"I remember you," She said. "When you were here before. You weren't much help to us then, if I recall correctly."

Ray kept his gaze level with hers. "I did all I could." Next to him, Carl went silent and watched as the two sized each other up.

Mrs Lowe took in a deep breath. "Well, Dominic is still dead, and you already caught the killer, right? I can't see as how I can be of any help to you now, unless he's out of jail already and killing innocent children again." Her voice cracked on the last words, and Ray spoke quickly and firmly.

"The killer is dead, Mrs Lowe. He was murdered. He's gone."

For a second or two, it looked like the woman was going to keep it together. Her arms tightened around her torso and she bit at her bottom lip, her eyes never leaving Ray's. Like a controlled demolition, however, her tower came tumbling down, in slow motion, as she just managed to croak out "He's dea..." before she was doubled over, clutching at her belly and bringing a hand to her mouth to suppress a sudden fit of retching.

Carl was up faster than Ray, and caught her by the shoulders before she could sink to her knees, half dragging her over to the sofa. Ray watched on numbly as Mrs Lowe sobbed and gasped for breath. *What the fuck am I doing here?* He thought, and knew it was certainly not for the pride and satisfaction of upholding the law. And, equally, it could not have been for the eventual payout, not always, and definitely not when he had visited this apartment before.

It took more than five minutes before Mrs Lowe

regained some kind of control, and to busy himself from his reeling thoughts, Ray had made her and himself a cup of tea (omitting Carl in his distraction). When he was sat beside her, and they were both sipping from the mugs cradled in their hands, it was only then that Ray ventured to say something.

"How old is your little one now?" he asked. "If you don't mind me asking."

Her eyes returned to meet his, and this time, there was none of the defiance and harshness in them. Only sorrow, but she still managed a very brief, very small smile at the mention of her daughter.

"She's eight."

"My Catherine is more than double that, now," Ray said softly. "You have to make the most of these years."

Mrs Lowe took another sip from the hot mug. "She'll be home in half an hour."

Carl cleared his throat and said they were sure to be gone by that time, but then she looked at Ray curiously.

"You came here," Glancing at Carl. "Both of you, to tell me he … that my Dominic's murderer was dead?"

Both partners exchanged quick looks. "Not exactly," Ray said, and shifted his position slightly. "I thought you would want to know. But, also, like I said earlier, you may be able to help us with something."

She continued to study his face, uncomprehending, before her gaze drifted away again. "Well, anyway, thank you..."

Carl cleared his throat and spoke next. "Where do you think your husband is, Mrs Lowe? You said you didn't know, but does he still live in the city?"

She looked curiously at him now, then back to

Ray. "Lawrence and me drifted apart, shortly after..." She began. "Well, he took it badly, didn't show up for work...I haven't seen him since christmas..."

Ray took a gamble and tried to press her, as gently as he dare. "Why do you say he took it badly, Mrs Lowe? Was he seeing anyone, a counsellor perhaps?"

She shook her head. "No, Lawrence was never like that...Well, he wouldn't talk to me, or anyone for that matter," She frowned as she tried to recollect, clearly paining her. "After a year, or was it two? He moved out, and...anyway, we rarely speak anymore..."

Ray had a flash of his own estranged wife and child. *When did I last call them?* He patted her arm reassuringly. "I Understand."

"Why are you asking about my...about Lawrence?" She started to stiffen and pull away from them both. The steel returned to her voice, and it started to rise alarmingly at the end of her question. "Is this why you're here? Is Lawrence alright?"

Another quick exchange of concern and Carl moved in closer, to speak as calmingly as he could. "We're not sure if its your husband we need to speak with, Mrs Lowe, but we would like to eliminate him from our enquiries. If he's safe and alright then then there's nothing to worry about, we just want to make sure that that is the case."

A bewildering indecision plagued her then, and Mrs Lowes' jaw opened and shut soundlessly as she considered different replies.

"You'd be helping Lawrence as well as ourselves, Mrs Lowe. I'm here because I owe you both that much." Carl leant back and regarded his partner at these words, but Ray would not meet his eye. "If you could tell us where he is, or anything you think that may help us find him?"

Her jaw set then, and she stood up and moved away from them. "Well, neither I nor Lawrence owe you anything, the way I figure it, detective."

Ray thought they had lost her, but then the woman slowly turned back round to face them. "I do have an old forwarding address for Lawrence somewhere." She said quietly. "He gave it to me shortly after he moved out. I'm not sure if that would be of any help to you now."

21

Howard Watts had learned to live with the politics side of policing, but he had never mastered it. Now, with such a narrow and focussed task, the phone calls he would get had become increasingly more ominous. He had a whole squad at his disposal and a generous budget, he was constantly reminded, and the location of one man, one in extraordinary fancy dress no less, could not possibly be so difficult, could it?

He was not particularly fond of the man Jameson, but Watts regarded him as professional and reliable in a sticky situation. He could speak openly around him, vent his frustrations, and Jameson could take it. When Watts entered the big meeting room, that was now permanently occupied by Jameson's team, there was no need to exchange pleasantries.

"Tell me you got something from CC control, Tom?"

Jameson led him to a screen in one corner of the room, on a long table with a row of laptops, printers and telephones. "It's not great, Howie. You know the area is not known for its security and neighbourhood watch schemes. We got a couple of captures, but it appears our man had some knowledge of the area. He took out a few of the cameras, we think with an air pistol, look," After clicking through some files, a grainy black and white video clip opened up, displaying footage recorded on one of the estates apartment block rooftops. As Howard watched, he saw a dark figure enter into shot and raise an arm. A moment later, the clip ended in an angry scramble of static, but Jameson closed it down and moved his cursor to another file. "We got a better one from the top of the corner store. We were able to zoom in and enhance the image."

Howard watched the next clip, and could not contain his surprise. "Jesus H Christ."

"I know, Lalonde confirmed that that was what he figured was happening, and we found the grapples, still attached. This kind of gear is not common on the high street, but shit chief, you can get anything over the internet these days."

The black and white clip, directed over the convenience store roof, happened to frame the building behind, and within the noisy grain of the enlarged image,

Howard observed what appeared to be a figure swing from out of shot and onto the top of the building, apparently suspended from some kind of rope. Howard slowly smeared a hand down over his face, and looked at Jameson grimly.

"You better have this network secured, and I mean airtight. We cannot allow anything like this to ever get leaked. Never."

Jameson was shaking his head. "Don't worry Chief, I got I.T. running firewalls and code on all this, it can't ever get out," if his words did not seem to lift his boss's doom-laden complexion, Jameson knew his next offering was not going to help either. "Forensics recovered this, Chief. From the Meadow's apartment. You may want to check this out."

Jameson moved to a cabinet behind them and removed an object in a clear plastic zip-lock bag and held it at eye level in the air between them. Against the light, Jameson invited the senior man to look closely and tell him what he thought it looked like.

"We dug it out of one of Meadow's henchmen. See the detail there?" Jameson pointed to the end of the heavy metallic object that fanned out from the shaft and tapered to a sharp point the other end. Howard frowned in consternation, as he marvelled at the absurdity of the words he himself was voicing. "Its supposed to be some kind of... feather?"

Jameson just nodded. "I'm pretty sure these things are less easy to get on the internet."

Watts shook his head in disbelief. "Please tell me this guy hasn't got his own brand of special toys and some kind of fucking utility belt!" His voice sound pained. "Next we'll be learning he really has fucking super powers."

A Commotion from behind them made Jameson and the Chief of Police turn around. Many of the team were gathering in front of the big TV screen on the wall, and Peters was in the process of turning up the volume. It was a news channel, and at the bottom of the screen, the words ‘breaking news’ were scrolling across while a familiar blonde reporter was busy composing herself and taking her cue from an earpiece. Howard’s frown deepened, as he cautiously approached the television and anticipated the next turn of events. He was certain it would be bad.

“This is Angela Draper for MBS News, live outside Glendale movie theatre on the East side,” Behind her, the blue light of a patrol vehicle illuminated the whole corner of the street, and an ambulance could be seen pulling away. just then, the door to the meeting room flew inward, and a particularly anxious young man looked at every face there until his eyes settled on Tom Jameson’s. “Sir?” he said. “We gotta report on ...”

“I know, Wilson, I’m watching it on the news now. You’re too late.” Jameson said gruffly.

The young man’s shoulders sank, as he turned to look at the television screen along with everyone else. Beside the news reporter, the camera was trying to frame a young lady who was pulling an overly-sized sports jacket around her shoulders and looking furtively into the camera lens.

“I didn’t know the guy, no. I just know he attacked me and tried to rape me. Was going to kill me, for all I know.”

“Could you tell us, in your own words, exactly what did happen to you? Did someone come to help you?”

“You got that right! My prayers were answered, it

was a miracle," At this, the camera zoomed into her face. "That scumbag was on top of me, tearing at my clothes, and I thought...I thought that was the end, you know? I thought I was done for, but then, this guy...he just swoops in out of nowhere in that crazy suit, and the next thing I knew, I was free and started screaming for the police. He was like a guardian angel."

"How would you describe this suit? Was it special in some way?"

"It was like something from one of those films, you know? With the mask and the boots and the, what do you call it?" The woman made a motion with her arms around her shoulders. "A...Cape, something like that. Looked like wings. I couldn't care what he looked like or what he wears, but for him, I can't tell if I'd be talking to you right now. He saved me, you know? Not like these god damn cops, they were no where to be found, and the one that does show up just looks at me like I'm some crazy street walker or some crap like that." Watts closed his eyes tight and prayed a meteor would hit the country right now, or some act of god could make this story just go away.

"Did he say anything to you, this winged man?"

"No, he didn't say nothing at all. Just swooped down and started whipping on this scumbag with some quick-ass kung fu moves and knocked him down to the ground. Made a mess of that guy, you know what I mean? He was the real deal."

The reporter turned to look out of the television as she thanked the woman and the camera zoomed into the reporters face till it filled the frame. She brushed a blonde curl off her forehead before she continued. "Could it be that Templeton has its very own superhero now? Protecting its citizens on the streets here, after night fall? This is the stuff of blockbuster Hollywood films, isn't it? But outside this movie theatre tonight, it seems that truth maybe stranger than fiction. In an exclusive we can share with you now, MBS believe they may have identified the winged vigilante, from a hack that was leaked onto this channels web page earlier today..." The picture changed to a web page with text, headed with the image of some kind of ancient warrior.

In the operations room, Howard snapped his fingers at Jameson and gestured toward a computer. The man took a second to rid himself of his fixation on the reporters words, and in the next instant, he had moved behind a desk and was hurriedly tapping in commands to the search bar.

"The conflict in Kurdistan has been much in the news recently, and no role in that war has been questioned more than the arms manufacturer 'Radcore'." Draper continued. "This industry giant has been responsible for the supply of many of the missiles and equipment used by both sides during the violence, and now, the contents of this leak make it clear who exactly are the major shareholders and investors in the company that finances Radcore, and some of those names may surprise you..."

Howard Watts imagined it would be easier to be a captain at the front line in Kurdistan right now rather than handle the shit storm he was looking at, and from his office, he heard his telephone begin to ring once more.

"...and the name of this mysterious hacker who claims credit for the sensational events of late," The screen zoomed in to the graphic above the list of names, and the shadowy, barbaric figure there with enormous wings framing his shoulders. "is given only as 'Icarus'."

22

Viktor Lenske studied his smartphone for an updated figure on his stocks performance that day, and did the calculation on the rise in its value. He nodded to himself with satisfaction, reached for his mojito and wandered on up to the wheel house. The deck of his yacht stretched backward in polished teak splendour, and beyond it, he could see the lights and traffic from the shoreline. As he watched, he noticed Pavel slowly strolling along the gunwhale to the stern, and smiled. He had selected his entourage well, and felt the security and assurance of a multi-million dollar expenditure on his protection.

The 'zheleznaya babochka', or 'Iron Butterfly', was anchored off the marina from downtown Templeton and only gently swayed on the unusually calm waters and light breeze that night. It was chilly, but refreshingly so, and Viktor took his fill of the cool air, while he finished his drink and watched the white shapes of seagulls gliding overhead like silent ghosts. If only his money could extend to finding a reliable woman, he reflected, as the frustrated Slavic cursing of his most recent acquisition drifted up to him from the lower deck.

He returned to the dining cabin to find Her stomping up from the swimming pool, hugging a robe about her and still cursing under her breath. She hissed something about the temperature of the water and started to mix herself a drink. When he suggested using the hot tub instead, she just snarled at him, which was not unattractive in her exquisite face. At six feet and in good shape for his age, with a thick pile of greying hair, Viktor still reflected that she would never be here without the abundant luxury he supplied. Like most things, put in perspective, he could live with it. Money may never buy happiness and perfection, but he was past caring. Success was all he truly cared for, and he pursued it ruthlessly.

His business mobile rang, and Viktor withdrew to his study to handle what was likely either a crisis to handle, or a lucrative proposal. He handled both the same way, with an easy, stoic clam that had been honed by years of experience. A passion for success was one thing, but it was never wise to be hot headed in matters of business and politics. The coolest, most intimidating characters he ever negotiated with, were the bigwigs within governments who had the most to lose and the furthest to fall. Viktor settled himself in a chair and reached across the mahogany desk for one of his favourite cigars.

At a little over fifty metres, the Iron Butterfly was a fairly modest vessel, with more traditional lines that Viktor had insisted on. It had a shorter bow than was considered fashionable, a wheel house somewhat closer to the fore, and the longer sunning deck at the rear allowed for plenty of space for fishing and diving. It meant fewer and more compact cabins, but Viktor Lenske wanted a ship that was practical as well as comfortable. If he had had his way, there would still be canons and a gunning deck in operation, but his lawyer had convinced him out of the notion. It still shipped a crew of ten, including his personal advisor and staff, and there was plenty of room for the further half dozen of his 'soldiers', as he called them. And because of its meagre size, if they drew anchor now, they could reach twenty knots in under a minute.

Each of his soldiers were equipped with an MP5 submachine gun, a proven firearm of which Viktor had an endless supply, and they were expected to carry them at all times. Pavel had his slung under his shoulder, his hand resting on the stock, as he made his third turn about the deck that night. It was quiet, undemanding work for the most part, which was credit to his boss's political manipulation and handling of his affairs. It was the benefits he earned from his loyal duties to Lenske that ensured his dedication. During these more languid times, Pavel would allow himself a cigarette or two, but strictly forbid any alcohol or drug use among his men. If there were ever an occasion when the political tide turned and his boss came under fire, they would be ready and more than capable of resistance. One of the advantages of working for an international arms trader.

The night sky that evening was clear; he could see the surface of the ocean, reflecting the moon, all the way to the shore, about five hundred yards away. As usual, the chances were himself and his team had another long, quiet night ahead, unless Viktor and his lovely young companion had a blazing row again. In his experience, that would occur about half a dozen times or so, before his boss would call it a day and look for a new companion. Not for the first time, Pavel wondered on the life of the rich and powerful, weighing up the advantages and disadvantages. He could certainly live with the luxuries and the women, but he was certain he would not be able to handle the diplomacy and politics, not to mention the exposure in the public eye. He only really enjoyed careers where you could openly carry a rifle and a pistol, and train to use them properly among a small, like-minded crew.

Pavel was halfway down the port side when he

heard it. A low bass thud against the keel. He stopped, tossed his cigarette over the side and leant over the rail. Using the spot light on the MP5, he aimed the barrel to where he thought he heard the sound come from. With his right hand, he retrieved a walkie from his belt and radioed in to Vassely, his second in command. A torch beam was searching the port side along with his scope spot, and between them, they picked out an object in the sea beneath them, low on the water.

A crackled response on the walkie prompted Pavel to bark an order, in Russian. “Alert Andrei, Peter and Nikki. Standby.”

The light showed an object cylindrical in shape, about three foot long and now floating passively away with the current. It appeared to be man-made, of some kind of plastic, and Pavel discounted the possibility of driftwood or sea debris. He heard someone shout up to him from a lower window, the owner of the torch, but before he replied, a thought struck him; If what they were looking at was intended to hit the ship, but not explode, then it was clearly some kind of diversion, and if the diversion had the effect of causing them to look down, then the danger was likely from… Too late, Pavel arched back to study the sky, his eyes hunting furiously.

All he perceived was the moon suddenly disappear behind some large black mass, and then he heard the metal cannister clunk on to the deck, followed by the hiss of the gas erupting from within. He sprinted in its direction, but before he reached it, the area was already filling with thick, impenetrable smoke, and the ships roll had moved the cannister out of his scrabbling hands. The next instant, he too was rolling over onto his back, as a heavy blow on his side knocked all the breath out of him and sent the MP5 clattering out of reach. He tried to grasp the butt of his pistol, to fire some warning shots into the blinding mist above, but another blow disabled his arm with a crack, and shattered the bone. A final blow to the side of his head sent him completely into darkness.

Having guided the drone over the deck, and slowing his fall with his wings, the man had landed into a stable crouch, and was able to kick off quickly to begin disarming the body guards. The first was relatively simple, with the advantage of surprise, but when a further two emerged from the gangway, he was glad of the smoke screen. They opened fire immediately, spraying nine millimetre rounds in his direction, about chest height. He felt a couple ricochet off his breast plate, and one nearly knock his boot out from under him, but once he leapt behind a rod rack, he could use his personal FLIR goggles to establish the best kill sites.

In the red and blue heat picture, he disarmed one with the nail gun and took out his knees, while the other dropped into a crawl and tried to scramble back into the wheel house. He moved forward with the tazer and taking aim at his lower spine, pulled the trigger to apply maximum volts. He only released the trigger once the guard had stopped moving, and stooped down to catch up his rifle. When the fourth guard burst out of the cabin door, he was already knelt beside the navigation table, and emptied the magazine into the confused mercenary. By his calculations, that meant there were two guards left, and they had no doubt mobilized to secure their boss and take up defensive positions.

The man thought back to the technical diagram he had studied of the ships layout, and opened the gangway door to toss down a second cannister, in the direction of the forward cabins. The mace started to fill up the area swiftly, but his breather was already secured over his mouth. Some of the lingering smoke and the stinging cloud of mace was obscuring the air, but he took the steps down to the cabin deck casually, dragging the soldier behind him by the heel.

From the dining hall, a guard emerged and began to fill the corridor with a deadly stream of bullets. Behind the armoured corpse of the fourth guard, held up in front of him as a human shield, the man used a semi automatic pistol to deliver several rounds into the targets chest, and the fifth mercenary slumped back against the wall.

He stepped over his legs, and continued down the corridor to the doors of the main cabins at the bow. He checked his progress when a man emerged on his knees, snivelling and sobbing, feeling a path for himself along the floor with his hands, blindly. One of the ships crew, the man waited for him to crawl a safe distance away, and then approached the far cabin door, reaching behind him at his belt.

In one movement, he slapped the charge on the door and depressed the detonator. Retreating several paces, he then squatted to his knees while drawing the protective wings around him to encircle his body, shortly before the detonation occurred. The noise was tremendous, and the concussion shattered the windows of the dining cabin and pushed him back onto his side.

Regaining his feet, he moved quickly toward the main cabin, halting suddenly when a fresh stream of nine millimetre rounds flew past his head. The last guard was crouched just beyond the smoking, smouldering remains of the doorway, desperately discharging his magazine in his direction, while screaming at the top of his lungs. He could see from the charred face that the sixth mercenary had suffered considerably from the explosion, so the man stooped and fired a fresh taser into his chest, paralysing him rapidly until the screaming had turned into a croaking gurgle.

Finally, entering the very end of the yacht, the man looked around the enclosure, now strewn with upended furniture and shattered glass. A soft whimpering drew him to the main dining table, which was like a large booth in one corner. There, he found a young blonde woman, who sobbed and cowered at the sight of him, trying desperately to retreat further back between the table and the seats. As he stooped over to look at her, shaking her head and drawing the nails of her fingers down the side of her face, he did not hear the door to the room behind him open, nor Viktor Lenske emerge cradling a shotgun in his hands. He turned just as the arms trader levelled the barrel toward him and pulled the trigger, the enormous blast making the girl scream aloud.

Instantly, one wing at his shoulder erupted in a cloud of scattered carbon shards, and he felt his rubberised skin pierced in several places up his side. The arm held in front of his face limited the damage done there, but the shock wave of the discharge rocked him back on his heels. With his other hand, he retrieved one of the steel feathers clustered on his belt, and slung it in front of him, toward the man in the doorway. The pointed tip embedded in the arm holding the shotgun, near the shoulder, and Lenske backed away in to the study again.

His senses partially recovered, but for echoes of the deafening shotgun blast, he advanced toward the room his quarry was using as shelter, wary and alert for another assault. As a precaution, he freed a four inch blade from a sheath at his ankle, and kept low to the ground. At the door to the study, he tapped at it until it swung open on the hinges, and found himself standing before the notorious arms dealer, a handgun gripped tightly in his fist and aimed purposefully at his centre.

Viktor Lenske was sweating, and mixed with the fear that was present in his gaze, The arms dealer was frowning in bewilderment. For a second or two, they regarded each other silently, and then eventually, the businessman snorted in something like derision.

"Of all the people who would wish me dead," Viktor spat out, in broken English. "For all the dangers I have lived through and bullets I have dodged, my end is at the hands of some...madman, in a fancy dress costume!"

Lips drawn back over his teeth in a bitter grin, Viktor remained sat while his uninvited guest stood over him, calmly, watching him. He took a quick breath, which he let out in a long sigh, and then Viktor turned the barrel of the gun into his own face. The man continued to just stand and watch, as the arms dealer pulled the trigger.

Only after the body slumped back in the chair did the man advance inside the study. It had been only about six and a half minutes since he had set foot on the Iron Butterfly, but now he took his time, as he cleared a space on the wall behind the corpse, and retrieved the small spray cannister from his belt. He wanted to be sure his symbol would be writ large and clear.

23

Raymond Knight had chosen an apartment high up, near the very top of the block, and did not regret the extra time it took in the elevator. In some way, he was trying to put some distance between himself and the squalor he observed every day on the street, and for the same reason, he kept his apartment neat and his routines orderly. He prepared his meals fresh, when he had the time, and the cooking helped keep his mind off work. After his meal, he would clean up, shower and prepare to sleep, and very little interrupted this routine. It was none the less welcome, however, when he answered the telephone and recognised the number of his ex. The time was late, he knew, but he still harboured the hope that maybe his daughter might be around to spare him a word as well. When he cleared his throat and settled himself onto a stool in the kitchen, he pitched his voice to sound formal and polite, careful to withhold any emotion from it.

"Good evening Karen, I hope you are well?"

"Raymond." Hers was equally distant, with the casual informality of a long time acquaintance, nothing more. "I trust I'm not keeping you from work, or sleep?"

"Not at all, dear. For what do I owe the pleasure of your call? Is Catherine there?"

"Oh, I was having a glass of wine more than I ought to, realised it was that brief column of time in which you were neither at work nor asleep, and against my better judgement found the phone in my hand. How long is it now, till you pack the job in, five years, six? Or have they sacked your ass already?"

Ray rolled his eyes. "Your wit was always a delight, my dear, I miss it greatly. You enjoying the single life, kicking your heels up at the singles bars? I'm surprised you're still indoors."

"No one could compare to you, my love," They both chuckled at this, but when they resumed talking, it was with an element of wary frostiness.

"Is it really only our daughter that you care to speak to, Raymond?"

"Of course not," Ray tugged at a loose thread at the knee of his sweatpants, awkwardly. "You know I love to hear that you're both happy and well. I can't visit as much as I'd like to, so I rely on you to keep me in the picture."

"Really, Ray? And just how much unspent holiday time have you accumulated so far this year, then? we're only an hour away, you know."

Ray groaned. "Come on now, Karen, don't lets drag this into an argument."

"Okay," she conceded, after a pause. "Seriously, are you keeping safe? You do hear some awful stories about crime on the news, and you're well past your prime, you know that." This got another eye-roll; It was said without a trace of humour. "Did you hear about the enormous gunfight at that gangsters hideout the other day? My god, I trust you weren't involved?"

Ray cleared his throat more conspicuously this time. "Of course not, dear," he managed to say, with some force of conviction. "You know they just have me pushing pens and filing reports these days. Its all paperwork." Ray lied. "So, uh, is Catherine out? She got a new boyfriend?"

Karen's voice came back over the line after a moment of silence, that was likely her analysing his words and finally deciding she was past caring if he was telling the truth or not. "No, she's here, wait a moment," In the background, "Cathy! It's your father."

Ray sat upright and adjusted his clothing self-consciously. It was rare that he managed to catch his daughter when she was not out on some date or concert or college event of some kind. She seemed to have less time to herself than he ever did, but all credit to his ex wife; she was very considerate on how he doted on his little princess, and had never resorted to using access to her as some kind of bargaining chip, like other ex wives he knew from work. Ray was grateful for that.

"Hello, dad?"

"Catherine, sweetheart, how are you? Why aren't you in bed?"

"Its Friday night, dad," after a teenage sigh.

"Well its great to hear from you. I hope to come visit very soon, maybe take you out for a movie?"

"I'd rather you took me out on patrol, dad. Run the sirens and chase some criminals."

Ray put on his serious voice. "Ah, I don't think that's such a good idea, sweetheart, its a dangerous placc out there, you know. You're much safer at home with your mother and studying for college."

"Not so dangerous any more, dad," His daughter said, suddenly sounding breathless. "Did you hear of the superhero guy, the one in the news lately? The guy with the wings, catching criminals and saving people on the streets?"

I only shot at the fucker! Thought Ray. "Uh, I'm not so sure he's the kind of guy he's made out on the news..." Catherine interrupted him. "Have you seen him, dad? Have you met him? I think he's wonderful!"

Oh, for fuck's sakes! Ray tried to keep the frustration out of his voice. "I wouldn't rely on him to save your skin, sweetheart. The police are out working twenty four seven trying to keep everyone safe, sweetie, much better to call them if you have any trouble, of any kind, you hear me?"

Another disappointed, disapproving sigh. "Oh sure, dad, I know, you're all the real heroes, I'm sure." Said with real sarcasm, but Ray ignored this.

"Just tell me you are keeping safe and not taking any risks with your life, that's all I care about. you know how much I love you."

"I know dad, night night."

Ray wished goodnight and other endearments into an empty line, as Karen got back on and informed him his daughter had left already. It was Rays turn to sigh this time, and he wished his ex a pleasant night instead. When he returned the phone to its hub, he sat back and studied the empty apartment around him, and quickly felt the walls of silence and isolation fill the vacuum. In hasty defence, Ray scrabbled for the television remote and pointed it at the widescreen on the wall.

Sometimes he would chance upon a classic old movie which would reliably console and amuse him, but more often than not, the television was so crammed full of craziness and unpleasantness, he simply found it annoying. He doggedly persisted in flicking through channels until, eventually, he settled on one that took his fancy. It was a replay on the UFC channel. Ultimate Fighting intrigued Ray, if just for the fitness and strength required by the combatants, but as a sport, he felt it pushed the label a bit far. Two guys, no rules, fighting till one passed out or would not stop bleeding, it was a bit extreme, even by modern standards of entertainment. Ray watched as an interviewer announced an exclusive clash later that night, and then spoke with, supposedly, the president of the UFC association.

“Take four corners...anywhere in the world,” The man began. “In one corner, they’re playing soccer, on another corner, they’re playing basketball, third corner they’re playing street hockey, and on the fourth corner, a fight breaks out. Where does the crowd go?...They go to watch the fight.”

It was a trite generalisation, but what with his daughters conversation earlier, it reminded Ray again of the fascination that the general population had with men of violence, particularly righteous ones who positioned themselves as ‘heroic’. Violence was sickening, uncivilized and frightening in its harm, Ray knew this from long, reluctant exposure. But, nevertheless, here he was, pitted against a one-man guerilla army, with all the backdrop of the criminal underworld for company. What a shit show, he concluded, and sank into his sofa to brood resentfully at his predicament. Acting on a sudden compulsion, he snatched up the phone again. It rang several times, but Ray chewed at his lip and waited until he got an answer.

“Carl? How’d you like to check out that address we picked up yesterday?”

24

Carl put up some initial resistance to his partners plan, citing the time of night firstly, but, as Ray guessed, the young man's eagerness brought him round in the end. The fact it was late and they would be unexpected might work to their advantage, and to top it all, Ray asked Carl to imagine bringing in public enemy number one, signed, sealed and delivered to the Chiefs office the next morning. That was all it took.

As Ray slowed the old Toyota outside Carl's modest two bed semi, his partner was already outside waiting for him. He could use a shave and a comb, but Ray was just pleased he had ditched the shirt and tie. When checking again the address Carl had written on a small piece of note paper, Ray decided it best to tap it into the sat-nav he had precariously glued on to the top of his dash. It was old, and cheap when he bought it, but it still seemed to work. Like the Toyota.

"You really think this could be our guy? Lawrence Lowe?"

Ray shrugged. "Worth chalking him off the suspect list. A list, I may add, that right now consists of one name."

Carl fidgeted nervously. "So, what are we saying here? A straight, upstanding family man has his son murdered, then goes loopy, puts on a suit and goes on the rampage? Is that really what we're talking about?"

Ray said nothing. After he turned down the slipway onto Milsom street, he spoke without looking over.

"You and Mrs Brooks have kids?"

Carl shook his head. "Mrs Brooks is keen, but I wanted to wait till I'm established in the department."

"You're a lucky man," Ray continued. "Kids are a big step, but you'll have a family then, and a home, and no man could ask for more."

Carl turned to regard his partner closely. "I guess you're right. You never married, old timer?"

Ray's voice dropped an octave. "Separated. Me and Karen moved up here from Hamilton nearly twenty odd years ago. We were happy, for a while at least."

Carl was wary of pressing a sore point, and tried to sound casual when he asked if his partner had had children.

"Yeah, we had Catherine a few years after we arrived. Your life changes then, and you change, but you have to find that out for yourself." Ray said seriously, meeting his partners eyes for the first time. "You cannot underestimate what a father would do for his child, Carl. You'd move the Earth, and raise hell itself if you had to."

Carl took the meaning silently, then to dodge the melancholy tone in the car, he added, "Where's the ex Mrs Knight now? You still speak?"

"Yeah, we talk. Our split was cleaner than some you'll lcarn about in the office." Ray gripped the wheel a little tighter. "We had a happy family for a spell, but I fucked it all up. Work/family balance; I could never get it straight. Kept too much to myself. A good wife is someone you can talk to, get stuff off your chest. That's important. You can't have secrets in a family, Carl."

Carl recognised this was all getting a bit too serious for his liking. "So, what your saying is, you pissed them off till they kicked your ass out," He said, with a sly grin. "By being a gruff old bastard. Who would have thought it?"

Ray chuckled, taking it in the good humour it was meant. He tried to think back, to when he was Carl's age, and if any one had ever tried to advise him in any way similar, on stuff like this. Because he certainly had not paid any attention if they had.

"You could be a good detective," Ray said, as the ancient sat-nav instructed him to turn left. "You'll make a decent living if you keep your nose clean and keep a cool head." The road seemed to end by a row of litter bins against a tall iron gate. "Just don't take your work home with you," Ray added. "And be sure to use all your holiday time."

They had parked beside a low rise chain of convenience stores that all looked permanently closed, and the general impression of the area was one of deprivation. Identical, featureless apartment blocks rose up into the night sky to enclose the space and seemingly entrap anyone who might make the mistake of trying to live there. Both detectives looked at the entrance ominously, before Ray turned to his colleague and asked him to wait, while he went in.

"Look less like cops, if one of us went up alone," Ray explained. "And if there is some kind of insane mastermind in there, I want you around to call in the cavalry. Just stay on the walkie."

He slammed the door and crossed the street to the gate. Ray imagined that even in broad daylight, the place would still look glum. There was no one at the shabby little welcome desk in the lobby, so Ray continued on to the stairwell, as if he were a tenant returning home. He figured room number thirty three had to be on the third floor, and right enough he found the flat and knocked gently on the door of the same number. For some reason, he was not expecting an answer, and after a moment, used the lock pick that every detective worth his salt knew to carry.

The room was small, very small, like a studio, and the décor cheap and tatty; thin linoleum on the floors, torn at the edges, and a couple of faded prints hung in tired frames on the walls. Even the plastic flower on the window sill had wilted. The cheap, metal single bed frame had a slim, uninviting looking mattress atop it, and in the tiny wash room beyond, Ray found an unwrapped tiny soap bar above a tiny sink, inconveniently abutting a low level toilet. There was no shower, and Ray wondered if there was a case for health and safety negligence here. He was surprised the living area had room for a two seater sofa, which he would never have trusted with his lower back, and a scuffed chest of drawers that was the only item of storage in the space. A television suspended on a shelf in the corner was of the fat, non digital kind, that could only be found in dusty used goods and charity shops.

This was like a throwback to the past, Ray concluded, and he very much doubted that anyone lived here, either now, or at any time in the last five years or so. *The proverbial shit hole*, Ray thought, then stooped to pull the sheet away from the bed. There was a depression in the mattress, which was was unusually clean, and the springs felt solid enough, at least most of them. And then, he looked closer at the chest of drawers, as something caught his eye.

The small picture frame positioned on top was not as dusty or as faded as the rest of the décor, and picking up the picture he studied the portrait of the young boy, smiling back at him. The colour was fresh and the quality of the print fairly new, and the features of the boy tallied with what Ray recalled from the case file on his computer. This was Dominic Lowe, and in the photo, he had obviously been caught off guard, in the act of playing with a family pet, and the wide grin he wore was carefree and blissful. A happy snapshot of time, that only a doting parent would find of priceless value. It was the only personal item in the whole place, and Ray guessed that it was all that was important to the absent tenant.

Ray held the photo, and could not stop looking at it and thinking. A happy child, the object of a parents love. He had many such photos like this of Catherine, and a frame much like this one on his bedside cabinet. The power of these images, of those memories, and of that feeling overall, it was enough to blur the corner of Ray's eyes, as he surrendered to the emotion.

What would he do? he asked himself for the hundredth, maybe millionth time in his life. To have someone rob you of that which was most precious to you, that meant more to you than your own life, what would he do? *Raise hell itself*, the words returning to Ray, as he replaced the photo and looked around the pathetic, pitiful abode, so far removed from the warm family home that he remembered from elsewhere.

And what had his man done, exactly, that was so bad? Removed from the community some human dregs that no one would really miss, nor cared about, least of all the institutions whom he worked for. Would he want to see this man rot behind bars for the rest of his life? *What the fuck am I doing?* Another familiar question, asked of himself a countless number of times. As if to compound the feelings that were testing his conscience, a distant wailing, of a child crying, came from one of the many flats somewhere above him. As Ray listened, it was followed by the slam of some door or object, and the desperate yells of fury of a person beyond their mental limit. How much suffering this building must know, Ray did not want to contemplate, he just wanted to get out of there, and turned toward the door.

Just as he gripped the handle, he glanced down and something caught his eye. Beside the frame was a small plastic litter bin, and within it, Ray noticed there was one solitary crumpled piece of paper, likely omitted when the bin was emptied. He bent over and fished it off of the bottom, unfolding it carefully in his fingers. It was a rental invoice, or half of one, as it had been torn into pieces before being binned. In small print along the bottom, the receivers address was still partially readable. Ray looked at it thoughtfully for a second or two, then stuffed it in his jacket pocket and slammed the door shut behind him.

Back in the car, Carl watched him as he climbed in, put the car into gear and pulled away from the street. It was not until they reached the freeway again that Carl felt he could no longer bear the silence.

"Well?," he asked. "Did you find anything?"

He noticed that it took his colleague several moments before he responded, and even then he did not look at him. "No," Said Ray. "There was nothing."

25

Watts had to act fast. As soon as he was informed of the incident, he feared the worst, and called coastal patrol to contain the waters within a two hundred metre radius and ordered a forensics crew to meet him there. He despatched a squad to control the port and grabbed Lalonde to accompany him as they left to oversee the operation in person. Jameson was left behind to man the department.

Even so, when Watts arrived at the parking area, he could see some reporters were already joining the crowd gathering by the docks main station. He swore under his breath and indicated for the nearest officers to curtail their advances. The focus of attention was plain, as a hive of activity was only dedicated to one purpose; Small craft full of officers were whizzing from the port to the stricken yacht offshore, or returning back from there, or simply circling round the giant, streamlined vessel, bobbing gently in the distance within a haze of light drizzle. The scene looked for all the world like a floating whale carcass, while smaller predators were clustering around to take turns feeding off of it.

Overhead, Watts heard the buzz of a helicopter, and prayed it was one of the departments that he had called in, and not one of the news channels. Following the aircraft as it swooped overhead and out to sea, he noticed the grey skies of that morning were not dispersing, and, in fact, seemed to be deepening into a more ominous shade, while the wind was steadily beginning to come on stronger. The very last thing he needed was a storm to scuttle the evidence.

"Is there any place round here," Watts indicated vaguely with his arms the wide births around the port, raising his voice above the noise and the wind. "Where we could tow that ship in under cover, somewhere private, and keep it under wraps?" This to the terminal manager, an appropriately bearded and warm-clothes-wearing, sensible-looking gentleman who considered everything carefully before replying. An officer called for Watts attention, pulling a coastal patrol man with him by the elbow. A brief exchange of words and nods, and Watts turned to Lalonde with a grave look of concern.

"They say it looks like our man." Lalonde absorbed this information with nothing but a blink of the eyes, and then offered to ship out to the yacht to take a look. Watts was half tempted to motor over there and take a look for himself, but swiftly shook his head and got on the radio. Nobody was to be allowed on board but the forensics team and the paramedic responders, he could not risk anyone screwing up what was there, no matter how unusual the circumstances. "Our main enemy is the weather, now," Watts said, looking back up at the sky, and then, as his gaze dropped, "and the press."

A large van with the news stations insignia emblazoned across the side pulled into the parking lot, and people started to empty recording and audio equipment from out of the side. Already, Watts could see the boom microphones emerging and being pointed at his officers faces. Other than the command to 'open fire', he struggled with the right order to contain this new threat to the investigation. Before he could come to his decision, another voice at his shoulder commanded his attention.

"What do you want us to do with the survivors, chief?" A burly, tired looking official, likely the coastal patrol captain, was indicating a small circle of distressed people, huddled in the docks makeshift staffroom. Watts brow lifted in momentary exasperation, then collecting himself, he managed to bark out for them to be taken directly to headquarters. "They're witnesses." he yelled, and then Lalonde brought his attention back to the water. He was pointing at the speedboats pulling up to the docks with various figures on stretchers, being attended to by paramedics, and more still on the floor of the vessels wrapped in body bags.

"What about the casualties, chief?" Lalonde asked. Beside him, Watts shoulders sank an inch or two lower, and he looked over to his right, to see mounted cameras being trained and focussed on to the macabre sight at the waters edge.

*

Ray couldn't taste the coffee, he just appreciated its warmth and familiarity. He could not coordinate any of his senses that early in the morning, and instead, let the television command his limited attention. The promise of a grey, wet morning outside his window did nothing to advertise the new day, and an empty fridge contained nothing of interest to nourish him. *Breakfast is for pussies anyway*, he decided.

He had actually finished late last night, or late for him; Headquarters was still busy at seven, as the night shift crews began to arrive and overlap with the staff putting in over time. Carl had even remarked on it, as he retrieved the jacket from the back of his chair and prepared to leave. "Its movie night tonight, and Mrs Brooks doesn't like me to be late," He said. "You trying to get in Watts' good books, or what?"

Ray had hastily dismissed the notion and joked about looking for other jobs in the classifieds, but when his partner had left, he could not resist looking over his shoulder to make sure no one else was observing his presence or listening in. Whether it was shame or guilt, Ray could not decipher why he felt the need for secrecy.

He had established that the business named on the bottom of the rental invoice he had found in Lawrence Lowe's apartment handled commercial premises in the city, and a further internet search had uncovered a contact number. Only once Ray was left alone at his desk did he pick up the phone and dial the number. He had had to cite his profession and authority to convince the person on the other line to give up the information he wanted, but in the end, he had been given an address which he scribbled on the back of a memo note someone had stuck on his computer screen.

As if to remind him of the occasion, right then Ray heard the muffled ring of his phone from the bedroom, where likely he had left it in the pocket of his discarded trousers, prior to collapsing into bed the night before. Quickly dismissing the notion of running in to answer it, Ray listened to the ringing come to an end and then returned his focus to the television.

A story seemed to dominate the news that morning, as similar images kept recurring on every channel he flicked through; a luxury yacht, emergency crew ferrying back and forth, and what looked like cadaver bags being brought to shore. It was clear some kind of accident or catastrophe had occurred at least, but it was not until Ray spotted the face of his department chief among the crowd did he start to sit up and tap the button to increase the volume, so he could hear what was being said.

When he found a channel with a reporter addressing the camera, and the 'live breaking news' slogan scrolling across the screen, he was not surprised to recognise the always lovely face of Angela Draper, from MBS News. She was looking particularly excited as she jostled with several onlookers and officers to make space for her piece to camera.

"...It is this reporter's understanding that police are treating this as part of their ongoing case on the winged vigilante who appears to have made this city his home, and what I have managed to learn from the police at the scene here are that there are several fatalities and injured. The word is of some kind of execution, given the person we know to be at the centre of the incident..."

Ray took a long pull on the coffee and turned the volume up louder. "Viktor Lenske," The reporter continued. "Was a notorious arms dealer and trafficker, whom we know to have been influential in supporting some of the more brutal and reviled conflicts around the globe in recent times. The associate of many dictators and corrupt rulers in some of the most war-torn regimes, he was moored in the yacht you can see out there behind me, awaiting the results of an extradition notice..."

On the screen they cut to a photograph of a rugged, middle aged man who was clearly the man being referred to. Ray watched transfixed, and shook his head in wonder as a faint smiled played about the side of his mouth. *You really went and did it, didn't you? you crazy son of a bitch!*

"Just a second... I believe..." on the screen, Ms

Draper looked out of frame while concentrating on the what was apparently being relayed in her earphones. "I'm sorry but we must go now to the studio, where I think we can bring you another exclusive...I think... a live stream is being broadcast, as we speak, on social media, and the person making the speech appears to be the subject of this investigation," The reporters eyes widened in apparent thrill as she comprehended the words she were giving voice to. "A man who has identified himself as the winged vigilante himself, the one calling himself 'Icarus'..."

Ray nearly fell out of his seat. On the television, a grainy and dimly lit vision filled the screen, of what appeared to be a man in some ancient armoury and a helmet. The image was framed to just below the chest, which was covered in a dark thick material, and over his shoulders, Ray could see the twin joints of what looked for all the world like giant wings, folded up behind him. Only his lips could be observed, under the main face plate and nose guard, as he spoke directly to camera in a gruff, husky tone. If this was their man, then all of Howard's efforts to keep the story out of the public's focus were about to be shot to pieces. Public enemy number one was on national television, declaring his guilt and defying his pursuers. Ray had to turn the volume up further to compensate for the poor sound quality.

"...the time of ordinary people living and hiding in fear has ended. Now is the time for criminals and those who do wrong to cringe in fear. Believe me when I say your time has come, because I am the one coming for you." The only perceptible movement from the extraordinary looking man, except for the mouth, was from gloved fingers that stabbed at the screen to emphasise his words. "At the dawn of civilization, Icarus Flew from the towers of the Labyrinth to warn others of the horrors at its heart. I have arisen again with a new warning for mankind; it is becoming nearly too late to treat the poison that is stopping the heart of our society. Unless we come together and defy our enemies, those that would harm us all, we will perish at their hands. They may claim it is for the benefit of that monstrosity they call The Economy, that sacrifices must be made to appease this beast, but I, Icarus, will not be fooled by their lies and their greed. Our enemies may be in positions of power, or hiding behind walls of gold while bathing in riches won from illegal wars, but there is no hiding from me. You can see today what I can do, not only to the petty thieves and bandits on the streets, but the wealthy corrupted traders in blood and sorrow. There is no escape from the hands of justice, and no expensive lawyers will play the system to keep them free. Retribution must be merciless, and apply to all those who poison our society, be they on high, or down low. We can shift the favour in our balance, have no doubt, and celebrate with me the day when those responsible for all man's woes realise their time has ended. For I, Icarus, will bring about their end, or die trying. There will be no other outcome. '

Ray shook his head in wonder, the coffee mug suspended in the air beneath his open mouth, getting cold, and heard his phone ring again from his bedroom.

Part Two

1

An ominous, thumping musical chord intrudes loudly, designed to recapture interest that may have waned at some point during the twenty-four-hour feed. An expensive looking graphic transitions from the previous theme to a subject that warrants its own logo, this one vividly depicted in large elaborate characters that read 'Superhero or Super criminal?'. The News anchor refers to another graphic, this time of a digital chart, showing a line slightly decreasing across a grid, and describes the implications that this chart illustrates. His grave demeanour tells of the severity of the situation, and to elaborate on the topic, he swivels in his seat to address the monitor behind him, which widens to fill the screen.

"I agree with you, Brian," Angela Draper is all wide-eyed anticipation, as she responds to the news anchor. "If the markets are a little shaky and unsure in these unprecedented times, then the same can not be said for the people of Templeton." The reporter is in the midst of a pedestrian high street, shoppers, store front promotional boards and temporary stalls filling up the background. "Those that work, live and buy their groceries here every day; normal, ordinary citizens like you and me," Angela continues. "Were happy to share their views on our new resident superhero with me earlier this morning"

The feed cuts to a series of clips, all no longer than about twenty seconds. The first is an elderly lady, dressed warm for the drizzly weather, and laden with several plastic bags. "I think its about time," She says firmly, a deeply lined and wizened face, that in no way compromise the steady, clear set of her eyes. "You never see an officer on the street these days, not like when I first moved here. It makes you think sometimes what you paid all your taxes for. It makes you angry, when you see what some criminals get away with. So, yes, I understand why this fellow on the television has had enough. At least he has got off his backside and is trying to do something about it, which is more than you can say for a lot of the younger folk you see these days."

The second person is a man of middle age, apparently caught between some engagement and keen to end the interview as soon as he can. "Well, what do we expect?" He says with a furrowed brow. "Our politicians seem content to do nothing but tell us what they think we want to hear, while only actually doing what benefits them and their friends. How many cutbacks have the police forces had to handle lately? I'm not surprised at all that someone has decided to take policing into their own hands. Who else was going to do it? I couldn't give a damn if international corporations are nervous."

Despite his eagerness to leave, the reporter behind the camera crams in a follow up question. "Murder?" The man repeats the last word of the question, as if it was an abstract concept. "Well what's the alternative? The prison system is clearly on its knees, and the courts seem to have their hands tied with human rights campaigners protecting the bad guys. These criminals have zero respect for society's laws, so why should this guy? All power to him, I say."

The third person is a younger lady in a loud dress, introduced as a university undergraduate, studying for an

Arts degree. “Ah, look, I think more and more people are getting fed up with how the world is run right now,” This with a wide, bashful grin. “Who are we supposed to look up to and idolise at the moment? The capitalists? The billionaires and governments who work for them? The world gets more and more random and bizarre every day, so I’m not surprised that fantasy is becoming reality. So what if someone wants to put on a suit and do some good? Why is it controversial that someone with good intentions has caused such a stir? Okay, he looks a bit weird, but I’ve seen weirder,” She pauses to giggle briefly.”And besides, we’re all about diversity now, aren’t we? Surely there’s room in the world for a superhero or two?”

Back on Angela Draper, and the reporter is now advancing along the high street, preparing to stop more people and quiz them for their opinions. “I have to say, Brian, that the people I have spoken to are overwhelmingly in favour of our new protector or defender or whatever this man ‘Icarus’ believes himself to be. This is a remarkable story that has captivated the public’s imagination and there seems to be no other topic of conversation...”

Angela Draper’s words were cut short as Jameson snapped off the television and turned to the crowd gathered in the headquarters training room. He was infected with the same resentful irritation and nervousness of his boss, and was gruff as he addressed the mix of newspaper and news channel reporters. He moved against the wall, beside the first row of chairs, and folded his arms as he watched those assembled prepare their recording devices, notepads and microphones, while those at the back levelled video cameras onto shoulders and aimed viewfinders at the hastily constructed plinth at the front.

“The captain is ready so take your seats people.

There'll be a statement and the chief will take half a dozen questions, no more."

Jameson nodded at the two officers at the rear of the hall to close the doors, and excited babble turned into low murmur as all eyes turned to watch Howard Watts come into view and take position at the dais and arrange some papers below the microphone mounted there. He had clearly changed into a clean shirt, probably fresh out of its plastic packaging, Jameson guessed, and noticed he had even combed his hair. He still looked like crap, when compared to the pampered professionals usually presented on news channels.

Howard cleared his throat, took a hasty swig from a glass of water and would only look up at the mass of reporters in sweeping, meaningful glares to emphasise his main points. The rest of the time, his eyes were downcast and busy following the vetted and authorised sentences.

"This department cannot tolerate the laws being broken or treated with flagrant disregard. As soon as people refuse to abide by everyday law and authority then our society and our safety is put in jeopardy, and our way of life comes under threat. Regardless of a persons background or circumstances, murder must be given the highest possible priority in law enforcement, and those guilty brought to justice. And make no mistake," A longer eye sweep tried to cover every face in the room. "We consider this man a murderer, and a serious threat to the safety of this city. I will not use the word hero when I consider the recent atrocities that have I have witnessed over the last couple of weeks. Nor do I appreciate some people in here sensationalizing and trying to paint this criminal as some kind of idol or gift to Templeton. It is no gift that rampages through our streets, brandishing explosives and bullets, destroying buildings and property, and it is only right that our forces are dedicated to the capture of this killer, and do our best to make sure he is brought to justice. I would appreciate if more of you would get behind us, in this effort."

Jameson scanned for reaction in the crowd, and grinned to himself. Everyone appeared to be listening with rapt attention, and, he suspected, he could see the odd trace of doubt and concern in some of the expressions, a rare thing indeed with these parasites. For all his reluctance and distaste at speaking in public like this, damn if old Watts was not pretty fine at putting his point across.

Looking back down at his notes, the Chief went on. "I have a task force working round the clock to identify and apprehend this criminal that calls himself "Icarus", and we will stop at nothing to end this man's campaign of terror. There will be no heed given to the man's words or credence to any message he may wish to deliver. If this man wants to express himself, he is welcome to do so at any conference or meeting like any ordinary decent citizen. Neither this city, nor this country, will pay heed to the demands and ranting of a confessed killer, committed to expressing his ideology using terrorist tactics. He is, in my eyes and in the eyes of the law, a wanted criminal, a vigilante, and no more, and I appeal to any one of you, out there, today, with any information or any knowledge of this persons identity or whereabouts, to do the decent thing and come forward, and help us catch this man, before he kills again."

On the prolonged pause that followed this sentence, an end to the announcement was presumed, and the hands of the amassed media flew up in one sudden imploring wave. Watts took his time to arrange his notes, take another swig from the water, and then eventually jab a finger at one of the reporters near the front of the pack.

"Are you saying it is this departments opinion that "Icarus" is some kind of a terrorist, and you intend to charge him as such?"

"I think I have made our position clear in that respect. Next question."

"What about the so-called 'victims', I guess you would call them, this Viktor Lenske, and, for that matter, Shaun Meadows. Were they not also wanted criminals? What efforts did your department make to apprehend these people?"

Externally, Watts did no more than set his jaw and take a second or two before responding to the question. Internally, Watts tried to mentally file the reporters image into his 'Beware' files. "I will not comment on cases currently open within this department."

"I think it would be fair to say their cases have already been closed, have they not? And not by this department, but by this so-called murderer you are prioritizing."

The reporter had to raise his voice above his colleagues beseeching calls for attention, which made his words sound all the more challenging. Watts locked eyes with the man, which was not easy as he was wearing spectacles, and his indignation radiated from his reddening face."Unless there are any more questions about this investigation," He said slowly and deliberately, "I am happy to bring this conference to an end?"

A new voice, female, yelled right from the back. "Does public opinion not have a bearing on this investigation? It would seem many of the citizens of Templeton are more tolerant of our man's behaviour, if not wholly supportive of it!"

Watts eyes narrowed as he sensed the effort in the room to undermine his message. He chose his next words very carefully, so as to give no chance for misinterpretation. "I give the general public more credit than that to determine who is or isn't a criminal and self-confessed killer."

With that, the Chief turned his back on the crowd and nodded at Jameson before retreating for the door back into headquarters. Jameson wasted no time in marshalling the three officers on hand to herd and compel, just short of using physicality, the thick squash of journalists towards the exits. Their pleas for more time and questions were stonily ignored.

2

The flesh of two kiwis, two bananas for thickness, and a mix of creatine and amino acid powders finished the blend that Icarus then raised to his mouth and poured down his throat. A fractured ankle was the worst of his injuries from the last endeavour, and a rigid brace supported that leg. Already, he could feel the injections and medication were taking effect, and the healing had begun.

The big drone was gone – only two micros

remaining – as was the heat sensor goggles. The smoke bombs were all used up and he had had to abandon the last of his tasers. Resources were dwindling, fast, and logging into a separate laptop, he brought up his currency exchange provider and instructed a transfer of thirty thousand dollars. This left very little left, he noted, and the thought occurred to him again that his operation may have to be accelerated or cut short, whichever was more financially viable.

Icarus booted up the online simulation game, 'City Surfer', and quickly selected a new avatar. In the guise now of a bikini model, he commandeered a motorbike, a ridiculous chopper with elongated forks, and drove to the innocuous looking block in the simulated city and approached one of the background characters. The agreed pattern of words were exchanged, and while the bikini clad blonde waited outside the apartment building, a stolen stretch limousine crashed noisily into a late night convenience store opposite. As she watched, two nuns scurried out of the wreckage, brandishing sub machine guns. Before they opened fire on the cop cars audibly approaching from nearby, a new avatar emerged from the apartment block. Although clearly King Kong, the character was no more than a head taller than Icarus's avatar, and he opened a text box and began to tap out his requests.

> **FUNDS ARE TIGHT. YOU HAVE ANY HEAVY DUTY, GROUND-TO-AIR BALLISTICS?**

King Kong responded quickly.> **I CAN GET YOU ANY FIREWORKS YOU LIKE, BUT IT'LL TAKE TIME.**

Icarus was insistent. > **THAT'S THE ONE THING I HAVEN'T GOT.**

In the games blocky, rough pixelation, the King Kong character raised his arms, in as much a gesture of a shrug as the game would allow. Further discussion convinced Icarus to consider what inventory his online supplier was able to deliver at short notice, and he mentally began to re-design his plans to fit around the available weaponry.

Removing to a different laptop, he was encouraged to see a regular repeat of his image and some of his words among the virals and memes circulating amid the social-cultural swamp of the internet. Manipulated graphics showed his visage, and sometimes only his symbol, over the photographs of countless public figures and politicians, warning of a day of reckoning. One had isolated a photo of a renowned billionaire, captured pulling a face to imply fear, and superimposed it next to his own image, and beneath, written the caption 'They will tremble'.

Opening his chat application, he saw with satisfaction that his profile had received over a million likes and subscribers, and many more profiles were emerging that were purporting to be his own. These fakes were useful, in that they added to the global conversation a similar message and another platform for the people to give voice to their concerns. The word was spreading, and the people were talking, and, hopefully, beginning to think.

*

At police headquarters, activity was at a stage that was just short of national emergency, or meltdown. More bodies than usual seemed to crowd the corridors and banks of desks, and the general atmosphere of urgency and bottled-up stress pervaded even thicker than usual.

There was no longer any need for an artists depiction of public enemy number one, and all the speculative paperwork of the last two weeks were torn down, and an enhanced and enlarged print of the man calling himself "Icarus" now adorned the centre of the wall in the task force room. During the seven and a half minutes of his live stream, he had been lit only by a small spot under his face, so everything behind him in the background was kept in darkness. None of the tech guys could recover any details, running the images through detection software, and only his appearance and voice were all they had to play with. Most agreed this was extraordinary enough, however, as the image burned in the back of everyone's brain that day was of a winged Grecian warrior, complete with full face helmet and nose guard, moulded chest plate and huge black folded wings, strapped across his back with some kind of black leather harness. In all, it made for a distinctly intimidating impression.

And it was this outfit that was the departments focus of investigation. Every armoury and military store, and every re-enactment and replica supplier, were to be contacted directly and quizzed about their clients orders. In addition, every other conceivable retailer of grappling hooks and climbing cordage had to be approached, and Templeton's emergency response department had to be raided to supply more telephones for the officers to utilize.

Those on research and profiling also had to comprehensively detail all the historical documentation on the original, actual Icarus, if ever such a person existed at all. Legends and myths had to be dug through, experts consulted and museum archives raided. This man chose Icarus for some reason, Jameson concluded, and he wanted to know why. In the meantime, No one trying to buy a military grade drone or heat-imager goggles in the last two years was to go unnoticed and unchecked, and some two dozen men were actively employed at head quarters working on just these tasks.

It was on this basis that Jameson was quietly confident that his man would soon be uncovered, and confided as much to the Chief of police. Howard Watts did not even dare fantasize that this may be the case, and instead, he chose to down-play their status, in a telephone call to Richardson that morning. He told him that their man had clearly made a mistake, a potentially crucial one, but stopped short on giving an estimation on how soon he may be picked up. The man's instability was clearly evident, Watts had informed him, and no fugitive so far detached from sanity had ever evaded authorities for long; history would back Watts up on that.

Nonetheless, he was well aware that now they had an identified suspect, more or less, that they were engaged in essentially a standard manhunt. Richardson had made Watts admit that much in their unpleasant conversation.

"You have all the city's resources at your disposal and, I take it, you do not lack for manpower?" The man had asked in that patient, reasonable, tone that simply oozed zero tolerance for deception or dishonesty.

"Nope, no, we're good for men," Watts replied, suddenly losing all appetite for the half eaten cheese and bacon roll that was cooling rapidly on a pile of papers on his desk. "It's just time we need."

A pause, and then, "Yes, well, time is a luxury none of us can afford to waste. You are aware, I trust, of the media interest in this matter?"

Watts confirmed that he was well aware, and then elaborated that it was all a matter of being prepared and waiting for that breakthrough, that one bit of decisive information. One thing he could assure his superiors of, however, was that he had the departments finest collaborating on the investigation, with all the latest technology at their disposal.

3

Ray did not get out of the aged, rusty Toyota. He just sat behind the wheel, the seat jacked backward. He had not said a word to the Greek vendor, just collected his chicken wrap, which he barely tasted, and mechanically chewed on it while staring out at the dirty grey waters of the Dunster.

He had made his escape the very minute his shift came to an end, a fact not unnoticed by some of his colleagues. "Must be six, Ray's off home!" Carlson had said in passing, and Ray quickly flashed him the finger. "If only he could draw a pistol that fast!" contributed another smart-ass, and Carl found it all very funny. "You trying to renew your relationship with that Angela Draper reporter?"

Ray put on a brave smile under the grilling, but really he was itching to get out of the building. Ian Fletcher, who was never one to miss out on cruel banter, posited that Ray was a 'Maverick' and a 'Loose Cannon' and that the media always loved such characters. This got the desired chuckles, but as the only one of them to actually see public enemy number one in person, Ray tried to shrug it all off by saying he had just been in the right place at the right time. Carl would hear none of it.

"The press are camped out on the street out there, begging for a name or a witness." Ray had noticed all too keenly the reporters and news vans outside the entrance to the car park on the way to work that morning. He had rarely seen them infiltrate round the back of the building like that before. "You have the look of an elderly, mature Stallone about you, I bet the camera's would love you!"

"Okay, that's enough for today, rookie." Said Ray, "I think I'd rather face down a junky's handgun than a T.V. camera right now."

Right then, a baby seagull stood on the edge of the river wall, about ten yards from where the Toyota was parked, and seemed to stare at Ray, as if trying to work out what he was thinking as much as the detective himself was. An adult flew past and the speckled, dirty-looking grey bird launched into the air, which made Ray look back down at the photo in his wallet. Catherine had been seven when they had taken this picture, and the carefree beam that radiated from her smile made it one his favourites. Every other tooth had to be missing, but to Ray it was more beautiful then he could describe, and he always carried it with him.

Catching bad guys. That was not what impressed her any more. There was a superhero in Templeton, and Catherine thought he was wonderful!

He closed the wallet, and this time Ray stared at the packet of cigarettes lying on the dash in front of him.

Yanni always had a few packets in the van, which he sold at a very reasonable price (for reasons nobody cared to ask) and looking at them now dragged Ray closer to realisation. Shame? Could this be what he felt? The world was a rough place, Templeton was a rough city, and he did his best to keep it clean, didn't he? What had he to be ashamed of?

It had been nearly ten years. Ten years since he had made lieutenant and his pay had gone up and the job had got harder and the paperwork had increased and his marriage had begun to falter. *And since you put Richard Darlow away.*

If the motions of his duties had become more automatic, and the ethics of his role had become slightly blurry, he tried to convince himself that it was not in the interests of the job to care, to let it matter to him. *Yeah, but he cares, doesn't he?*

Anger flushed over him, and he crumpled the cigarette packet in his fist and tossed it out the window, then he stared intently at the water flowing away towards the sea, carrying countless items of discarded waste and litter along with it. *You can't save the world, one man can't do that! A whole department of cops can't do it!*

Ray took a long breath, shut his eyes and then pulled out the crumpled memo note from his jacket pocket, staring at the address scrawled in his own slanted, clumsy hand writing. It was nothing, he told himself, what did he care if their man was hiding out at this place or not? So, Ray asked himself, why had he not told Carl about it?

He looked again at the address on the paper, pictured the area and calculated how to get there. He could call Carl, explain what he had done and ask him for his backup now. Would take ten, maybe twenty minutes. But Ray was not going to do that. Carl was not so bad, he may even grow to like him, but for now, Ray turned the key in the ignition and aimed the car back toward the city.

If some decision that he and the department had made, long ago, in accordance with routine and best practice, had been mistaken, and if it was the case that now their error had somehow festered and bled out into the present, in the form of a deranged nightmare blowing up the city, then he wanted to see for himself, first. If only to confirm that life really was that fucked up, and it looked like he may be the one to pay the price for it.

4

Of all the desks in the crowded and poorly ventilated task force room, Nick Guyler's was perhaps the most calm and uncluttered. It was just himself and two massive monitors, which were divided into numerous windows, and all of them would rapidly swap around in preference of his attention. As the head of the virtual police forces, Nick's job was really just to oversee the minions of computer and tech staff who were equally calm and immersed in their computer screen enquiries, at other desks around the real, brick building. While Watts' officers were looking for their man in the sunlit, chaotic and odorous real world, Guyler and his team were searching for digital traces of Icarus in the dark, murky virtual world of the web.

Jameson explained this, in somewhat plainer, simpler words, to his own overseer, who stood beside him looking down warily at the big twin monitors. Watts was baffled as to what his tech staff did, how their manipulation of a computer keyboard could unlock data vital to investigations, but he tried his hardest to hide it. He expelled any glimmer of wonderment from his face at mention of the number of databases they had accessed and the latest decryption software they had employed. A nod and a low grunt of approval was all that Watts offered, while his operation head asked 'the computer guy' for an update.

Nick revolved in his seat, and smiled at his Chief, making his cheeks and eyes wrinkle and betray his middle age. Otherwise, the glasses and unruly mop of blonde hair portrayed a more youthful man, one who radiated intelligence and that calmness that came from grappling with a very complicated and tricky digital cohort that required lots of patience. Watts asked him about Icarus's web posting site.

"Any time you log into and use a website you leave a footprint, one that can potentially be followed and tell us something useful about you." Jameson offered.

"Yeah, but equally, for those who are a little more digitally savvy, shall we say, it is equally possible you can sweep clean those footprints, or at least conceal them from view." Guyler interjected. Watts frowned and pressed his man further, with a comment that he hoped was at least relevant.

"He's visible all over the web, we got his mug shot

right there on the screen, and we know its him, it can't be anyone else."

But this just got a wider smile from the tech department head, as if patiently indulging a young child learning basic Math. "Yes, but its all about the server, Chief. The site that is hosting this social chat forum is defended and reinforced with more digital encoding and firewalls than the whole countries police forces combined, most likely."

Watts could not conceal his incredulity. "But, how can this guy access this kind of protection?"

"Often, this protection is routed through Switzerland. Obviously, they are not legally bound to disclose to any state regulator, and their neutrality is maintained for big business and, uh, political skulduggery, shall we say? There's a lot of very rich guys out there who would rather people were not able to trace where every dollar came from, or political parties who would rather people didn't know where all their international donations went to. Switzerland keeps it servers deep under ground, in every sense, and if you were to crash into their systems you would probably crash a healthy number of major banks and governments all around the world."

Watts knew when he was out of his depth. He looked to Jameson and saw no enlightenment forthcoming there. "So, what, there's no way to pin down our guy?"

"Not in any quick or easy way, no," Nick Guyler responded, circling his attention back around to the big twin monitors. "But there is still a variety of tactics that may be useful as subscribers to his blog. We can try antagonising and provoking, hopefully to get a response that might provide some insight"

"Like the Agent Provocateurs our friends in the

secret service employ," Jameson added with a sly wink to his boss. "I don't see why we shouldn't get down and dirty like the government boys do."

Watts grunted his approval, then leant forward and placed a hand on Guyler's shoulder. "This 'blog' as you describe it. How is it sitting with the public? I mean, is it popular?"

Guyler grinned. "Its got nearly two million subscribers so far. I'd say that's pretty popular."

"Two million?" Watts face fell, before he cleared his throat and spoke in a lower, more confidential tone. "It wouldn't hurt to sow some seeds of, ah, disagreement and, maybe, outrage, you know what I mean? Lots of seeds."

The Tech whizz nodded, and opened up a comms window.

"We want to dilute some of this hero worship that's coming out, particularly this use of the word 'superhero'," Watts continued. "I hate that word. Try tossing some alternative phrases about, like murderer, lunatic, racist...anything like that."

"Throw some shit around," Jameson agreed. "See if it any of it sticks."

*

Unlike previous nights, it was not raining that evening in Templeton, but still, the dark skies, stagnant air and drifting patches of smog preserved the city's unwelcoming aspect, reinforced by the constant drip and patter of neglected guttering and pipework in the Shoremouth estate that made it seem like it was raining, anyway. Shoremouth was that part of the city that stored all the supplies and received all the produce that kept the population, and just barely the local economy, sustained. Enormous cargoes emptied out onto the dockyards not more than a block or two away, and a steady stream of lorries and trucks rolled in off the highway to unload and get loaded up again. Everything that kept the city alive entered the maze of vast, faceless depots and warehouses in this upper reaches of the city limits, and Shoremouth constantly regurgitated its riches, day and night, never resting or sleeping.

At the centre of the estate, there were few signs of life, other than the hiss and whine of machinery and vehicles, somewhere behind the enormous blank walls that were duplicated pretty much everywhere Raymond looked. There were one or two lights here and there in windows around him, the occasional gaping entrance as a lorry backed inside, but otherwise, it was almost impossible to tell one building from another. He recalled some speech on television of the mayor promising to invest in regeneration of the area, but it was clearly too late now. To disrupt the established dynamic and function of the area now would bring all of Templeton grinding to a halt.

Parked outside a unit that appeared somewhat smaller, given the enormous installations that stretched out of sight either side of it, Ray paused and checked the now smudged ink of his handwriting once more. He was on the right street, he concluded, but names and numbers of buildings were largely absent and redundant around here. Looking back at the tall twin doors and featureless sheet metal facade, Ray felt a queasy discomfort tug at his insides. As if the lack of imagination on the outside made the brain compensate with creative alternatives, his every nerve was set on not going any closer to that building, and certainly not inside it.

Ray had to force himself to leave the warm comfort of the car, and for the first time truly contemplate what he was attempting, with the stark reality facing him large and lurid. On an impulse, he ducked back into the Toyota and reached over to flip open the glove compartment. Inside, he withdrew the thirty eight calibre snub nose revolver, and, after checking that he had remembered to re-load it, he tucked it into one of his jacket pockets. The heavy chunk of metal did little to reassure him, but nonetheless, Ray approached the big twin doors of the commercial unit.

A heavy chain and padlock indicated there would be no easy entry granted to him, and Ray wandered further along the building until he came to a regular sized door, that was only visible in the dim light of an adjacent premises by its outline against the sheet metal. On testing the handle, he found it was locked, but after a furtive look around over his shoulder, which was entirely unnecessary in the desolate gloom, Ray inserted an old service-issue pick into the lock beneath the handle and forced his shoulder up against it. The door gave under his weight, and Ray stood looking into the shadowy depths of the warehouse beyond.

5

Knight waited in the doorway. There was very little noise from within, so the noise of his breaking in must have been heard by anyone that happened to be inside. Taking a few paces forward, Ray punctuated his arrival with a call of hello. He had to clear his throat first of all nervousness to make the sound loud enough to travel through the wide, cavernous space.

The only illumination was from a strip light, partially concealed in the mezzanine built into the second half of the space. A metal gangway led up to this area, and beneath it, in the thick gloom, Ray thought he could make out the shape of a large van. Other than a few discarded boxes and a couple of steel tubs plumbed along one side, some odd, hanging cordage and some heavy duty brackets, there was nothing obviously incriminating that Ray could identify. Was that a punch bag hanging in the corner?

A low, digital hum was the only sound audible in the enormous enclosure, and this seemed amplified in the silence. If Ray had been fearing some furious attack or explosive booby trap, he appeared to be wrong, and was very grateful of that fact. Before he dismissed the notion entirely and abandoned the whole exercise, he advanced forward toward the steps to the mezzanine area. If there was an innocent reason why a light, and possibly a computer, was left on and running, then he would call it a night, and go home a very relieved man.

To complement the sound of his footsteps rising

up the stairs, Ray called out another 'Hello', just in case, before he crossed the door-less frame and entered the mezzanine area. The strip light was some kind of blued, ultra violet installation, and the digital hum was coming from a long desk dominated by two large monitors, blinking on standby. At an angle to the desks was a work top that stretched along half the length of the area, with various tools and equipment evident, while a large television screen was mounted on the wall behind. Ray paused in the entrance, as his eyes roamed the space, and tried to comprehend the significance of what he was observing.

A short distance from the desk, a tripod was fixed to the ground with a video camera mounted on top, and in the corners of the space, great cabinets were installed housing unusual items of moulded steel and what, as Ray squinted harder, appeared to be propellor-driven flying craft of some kind. Another cabinet appeared to house an array of weaponry and military hardware. The whole effect was one of busy industry, and once Ray had stopped looking for detail and finally acknowledged what he was looking at as a whole, the picture became suddenly very clear. His skin prickled and his breath caught in his throat, and turning his back on the scene, Ray fumbled desperately in his pocket for his phone while trying not blow the top of his head off with the handgun. He had found Icarus's base of operations.

Ray managed to awaken his phone and thumb the icon for contacts. At a run it was hard to operate the phone and get the right number, but after several hissed curses, a fortunate thumb jab brought up Carl's number and connected his call. At the bottom of the stairs, he got through to an answer message, and with another barked curse, growled out his words breathlessly.

"Its him. Carl? We got him. Forget what I said to you before, I'm standing in Icarus's place right now." He had covered half the distance back to the door, when he felt an enormous shove above his right hip, which sent him slamming face first into the side wall panels, making the whole frame of that part of the building rattle on its rivets and bolts.

Falling backward over two wooden pallets, Ray rolled over onto his chest and lay there for a moment, trying to suck some air back into his lungs from the dusty floor. His lower vertebrae screamed from the blow and the bridge of his nose throbbed from the impact with the wall. As he climbed up to his knees, he just had time to register the rushing black form of his attacker, swooping down upon him. He tried to raise an arm to deflect the inevitable blow, but even before his hand left the ground, the punch came. It hit Ray with such force, it flipped him over onto his back.

His hands clawed at the hard concrete to control his momentum, and when vision came back to him, all he could see was the dark recesses of the ceiling. His neck had snapped round in the opposite direction, and when he painfully turned his head back in the direction from the where the attack was coming, he saw the figure approaching him again. It looked impossibly tall, and as dark as the shadows that framed it.

A falter in the motion. An almost imperceptible stagger in the stride of the spectre that was rushing forward, and Ray mustered a desperate hope. At the moment the assailant arrived to deliver the finishing blow, Ray raised his knee and kicked out with his right foot as hard as he could. His shoe struck the limping leg with a glancing skim of the heel, but it was enough to topple the shadow and bring his weight crushing down upon the splayed detective.

Entangled on the floor now, the two men writhed with furious urgency for supremacy. His assailant was clothed in a rubberized suit that made it almost impossible to grip, and gloved fingers curled into a claw strained to sink into Rays throat. He managed to clasp his hand over the spectres wrist and he pushed with all his might to try and redirect the thrust into the air. Instantly, Ray surrendered his supporting arm to get a hand under his attackers chin, and push the gnashing jaw upward. Fingers now moved to his wrist, and squeezed the veins there. Rays only hope was to loosen his other hand and get a blow into the exposed wind pipe, but that hand was pinned to the ground. In that feverish moment of exertion, he felt that their strength was a match, but the relentless force of his opponent Ray just knew would never end. His stamina would fail, while this man would never tire.

Finally, Ray let out his breath and in the moment his muscles slackened just a little, he felt the weight shift above him and his opponent wrestle all advantage away from him. He kept his eyes firmly closed as the explosion of force impacted his skull and he sank painlessly down through the floor and into the release of total blackness.

6

Carl Brooks arrived early to get a half hour in at the gym. Never one to smoke, and with no real appetite for alcohol, Carl's fitness took up the most of his spare time. The dangers of the job were very real to him, but he was determined to supplant any fears he may have by becoming as large and solid as he possibly could. No one would ever mark him as a pushover. Completing a twenty minute tricep routine, he now warmed down on the punch bag. He swung his fists as fast and as hard as he felt his body needed, letting his muscles and his testosterone guide his hands, with as much energy as he needed to expel.

After a quick shower, he made the journey to his desk, feeling refreshed, and woke up his computer. He placed his mobile next to the keyboard on his desk, and noticed for the first time that there was the symbol for a voicemail in the top corner. He found himself undecided how to divide his attention between the numerous emails waiting to be opened, many of them red flagged, and the phone call that was more than likely some pointless spam message. In the end, he continued to stare at his monitor as he brought the phone to his ear.

A few seconds later, the computer monitor suddenly out of focus, Carl's eyes dropped to examine the phone in his hand, still able to hear the feminine robotic voice asking if he would like to repeat or delete the message. He looked at the empty desk beside him, and sat there for some time, mentally weighing up all his options and all the potential consequences. Eventually, he put the monitor to sleep and rose to his feet.

Looking around headquarters right then, he could see everyone was suitably occupied, so much so, that he could pretend the message he had just received had never happened, and no one would be any the wiser. Officers, agents and staff of all kinds were engaged in purposeful conversations or hunkered over computers, hailing one another over fibre-board divides, just like any other day. Only, if what he heard was accurate, then all this would be turned upside down.

Carl proceeded stiffly to interview room one, a sudden heat from within making his head feel warm. Pushing open the door, he saw Jameson bent over an officers shoulder, listening intently to what was being said. Everyone else in the Ops room were so occupied with their tasks that no one acknowledged Carl's entry or his being there at all. He had to raise his voice to be heard over the thrum of numerous hushed conversations.

Jameson looked up at Carl with a frown. "What is it Brooks?"

It was too late to turn back now, Carl thought. "Uh, Its about the assignment me and Ray were working on. I think, uh, we may have something …"

Jameson stood suddenly upright and covered the three paces to where Carl was standing in one swift, fluid move. At such close distance, so that Jameson had to look up at the bulky detective, it was almost laughable to Carl that the man may be trying to intimidate him, but nonetheless, he still felt uncomfortable. By now, half the task force had stopped what they were doing and in the ominous hush, it was clear everyone was trying to hear what was going on.

"I gotta phone call," Carl continued. "I think something's happened..."

Jameson's narrow, angular face screwed up even tighter, while Carl could feel the hostile eyes probing into his mind. "Its Knight, isn't it? What the fuck has that guy done now?"

This felt like it was going about as badly as he suspected it might, so he just let all the words spill out. "I think Ray may have found our man. Icarus. At least, that's what he tells me. I mean, that's what it sounded like."

Jameson's face remained a frozen image of incredulity and indignation. There was a pause for a heartbeat or two, and then Jameson spoke.

"Where is he now?"

*

The images were always the same. It was a crazy blur of violence, directed at him, from a man entirely in shadow, almost as if he were made of that shadow. The terror was tantalizing, the desperation only ever intensified, and the fight would never end, in his mind. It tormented him, challenging him to escape the loss that always ended the contest. The pain of the final blow to his skull kept repeating at the climax; a slam, the explosion, and then darkness. And again the impact, the pain, the blindness, over and over, until the pain was unbearable; a constant throb that dragged Ray slowly up out of unconsciousness.

When eventually he opened his eyes and blinked

them back into focus, the only thing that remained of his mental battle was the feeling of hopeless desperation, and the pain. It throbbed about the back of his head like a heavy iron clamp. It was only after he tried to get to his feet, that a fresh pain in his arm forced him to think about where he was, and what was happening.

The room was oddly familiar. Odd, because it was not one he had ever lived in, and one he knew had never been feature in his life, or anyone else's he was familiar with. But he knew he had been here before. It was Lawrence Lowe's apartment.

The sound of a key in a lock and the door opening cleared his mind of the last of the fog, and brought his senses to alert. A man had entered the room and was stood close to him. Ray could not see the man, as he was positioned behind him, while he was sat in a chair, bound in position by tight, unforgiving cordage, that seemed to be cutting into his skin. He could feel the man behind him, watching him, and to end the thick, uncomfortable silence, Ray opted to speak. His voice was almost unrecognisable.

"I know you, don't I?"

"And I know you. You are police. A detective. We have met before."

Ray swallowed, trying to get some moisture back into his throat and make his voice sound more normal. "When I met you, you were called Lawrence Lowe."

"I don't recognise that name any more. That man is not me."

"I met a very upset mother, with a much-loved young daughter, who would disagree with you."

Feet circled his chair swiftly, and the closeness of another warmed the side of his face. Icarus leaned into his eyeline, making it impossible for Ray not to look up and into those fierce eyes. It made the breath catch in his throat.

"You don't talk about them, you understand me? Never."

Ray took a ragged breath, and tensed himself for what he guessed would come next. "And Dominic?" he asked.

The hand flew out so quick he could not tell if it were the left or the right. It was a slap, but swung with such fury, it whipped his head to the side, leaving a sharp sting on his cheek and making the crick in his neck flare with fresh agony. When he breathed out next, it was one slow, staggered hiss.

The voice came loudly and was dripping with venom. "Say that name again and it will be the last word you ever fucking utter!" For an uncomfortable few seconds, they remained in an electrified silence, while Icarus fought with the urge to say more or strike the detective again. In the end, he stopped seething over him and turned, stepping away to the window. The light there was dull but still indicated daylight. Ray tried to listen for the sound of traffic or any other noise that resembled normal life; any reminder of a safer, saner world. His captor was not wearing the armoured helmet, nor the heavy wing attachments, but the man's presence was intimidating enough.

"It was your job to find his killer, to stop him before … before he … "

"We got him. We may not have super powers," Ray spoke between gasps. "...And we have to work within the law. You can't..."

"The law set him free!" It was a roar. "How can a man like that ever share the same free air any of us breathe? Ever walk the same earth beneath our feet? He was a fucking monster, an abomination!"

"We had to deal with him, negotiate … we had no choice, there were other children," Ray raised his head to aim his voice more directly at the figure pacing the floor in front of him. "There were other parents. Parents just as upset and distraught..."

"Don't talk to me about upset and grief. Don't talk to me, don't even fucking speak. You have no idea..." The seething resumed, while Ray felt the man was selecting his next words carefully.

"You failed. You are a failure in your job and you do nothing to serve this city, to protect its people. You are a disgrace to your badge and to man kind," Ray recoiled from the accusations, not only because of the truth they contained, but also because they indicated he was going to lose this verbal battle, as well as the physical one, and the consequences of that could be fatal.

Icarus continued. "I will not allow you to get in the way of the work I am doing. You do not deserve to be called a crime fighter, and you do not deserve to waste any more of my time. You will not be missed."

7

Watts entered interview room one at a fast trot, and his eyes hunted down Jameson immediately. "Talk to me, Tom," the Chief of Police said, taking in the somewhat sheepish figure of Carl Brooks beside his head of operations. The rest of the crew in the Ops room were already jabbing at keys furiously, hissing desperately into their mobile phones or dashing for the door. "What have you got?"

Jameson nodded at Carl. "Your man tells me he and Knight were running a re-con on their own time, and he thinks Ray may have bumped into Icarus himself."

Recovered of some of his wits, Carl found his voice and squared his shoulders in defiance. "We were just following up on some names of victims relatives, from the Darlow case," Carl continued with a pointed look toward Jameson. "As we were instructed to."

Watts seemed incapable of doing anything but blink rapidly, but then he snapped out of it. He glanced at Jameson. "Weren't we supposed to be notified on any possible leads?" Jameson nodded once in affirmation. "Yes," He said, his eyes fixed on Carl's. "We fucking were."

Watts looked back to Carl. "What happened?" It was obvious his answer had to be delivered in a second or less, or there would be dire consequences.

"We got an address. I thought it was nothing, but then Ray called..."

Watts interrupted. "We got a squad prepared and

ready to go?" To Jameson, who nodded again. It felt like everyone was on the point of exiting the building and hitting the sirens. Back to Carl, "Knight. Where is he now? You said he may have found Icarus?"

Carl swallowed. "That's just it. It sounds like our man may have found him, too."

*

The only thing that implied in any way that Ray may have some hope of surviving this encounter, was that Icarus had not chosen to kill him already. It would have been all too easy to finish him off at the warehouse, then dispose of his body in the Dunster, but he had not done that. He had dragged him up to this room and into this chair and returned to decide the matter. He studied the face in the failing light from the grotty window. Defined cheek bones, a strong jaw, it was the intense blue eyes that were immediately noticeable, however.

"Killing a cop," The croaking voice did not sound like his. "You think you can live with that?"

The figure did not move, and the words came after an uncomfortably long time. "My feelings are not important. This is sentiment, its not relevant."

"I have a wife and daughter, too." Ray tried his best to keep the desperation out of his plea. Keep it neutral, passive. "...And just like yours, they will miss me. It's important to them."

An arm raised in the air with violent swiftness. "Do not play with my emotions, detective. I have none."

"My daughter is obsessed with you, she loves you, so do many people her age." This said with more dejection and defeat. Ray could not hide that from his voice. "How do you think she will feel when she knows you murdered her father?"

"Sentiment."

"Its murder. You are supposed to be a super hero. You were supposed to go after the criminals, to kill the bad guys."

"SO WERE YOU!"

Ray's head dropped. Icarus had moved behind him again, and when he spoke, his voice was harsh and rasping with spite. "But you don't, do you? You fucking cops, obeying your laws made by the rich and the powerful, chasing down the poor and the desperate and turning a blind eye when the real villains suck out their money and their power and leave everyone to suffer. Just victims to them, to you. Poor, hopeless victims, with no one to protect them."

"I wanted to kill him."

"Who?"

"You know who. I couldn't bear to look at him, at the end. I wanted to kill him." Ray tried to crane his head around, over his shoulder, all attempt at bluff and trickery abandoned. Now he was simply confessing. "I couldn't, no matter how much I wanted to. It was my job, and I hated it." With the effort of saying these things, his head dropped again, with the tiredness of putting up with pain, fear and now shame.

"If you're gonna kill me, get it over with." He mumbled.

Icarus stood, still and silent in the little grotty room with the detective for maybe another twenty seconds, half a minute more. Then, he moved swiftly to the door and left the apartment, locking it behind him.

8

Lucinda Watson had risen through the ranks with hard graft and determination. She made no issue of her sex or her youth, and dressed appropriately and smartly, always bearing in mind her late father's mantra about looking and feeling successful to become successful. It was only when she entered the realm of politics that she found herself up against an impenetrable wall of established hierarchy, operating largely through nepotism, as far as she could tell. She did not allow this to dampen her ambition, and instead proceeded to carve a place for herself in this wall, which came to fruition one day, she knew instinctively, when a renowned, elderly gentleman congratulated her on her 'discretion' and commented that 'she would go far'. Now, at the age of forty five, she was one of the youngest state representatives to hold the office, and she threw herself at the job with a conviction that impressed and intimidated her peers.

It was not easy; the chaos of balancing the needs of the establishment with upholding the image in the public eye, and the unregulated crises that threatened to swamp the district on any given day. Every morning now she seemed to awake to a fresh new blizzard of strife that seemed sure to bring society toppling to its knees, but she knew better than to hope for help from higher authorities, the upper echelons of the establishment. It was on her shoulders alone to keep the state from collapsing, or at least disguise any collapse from public awareness, and she dutifully projected a smart and resilient exterior while all around her crumbled.

This month, it was some mad man in a costume, which should have been small fry compared to the hazards Lucinda observed looming on the horizon. Nonetheless, somehow this freak had managed to tap into some well of public feeling, and now the entire system of law enforcement was under scrutiny. It astounded her how some tiny thing could escalate, and she was reminded of one wizened ex colleague, on the eve of retirement, who confided in her once upon a time. "its not the big, dirty scandal that can undo you," he'd said, with a hint of a smile and a twinkle in his eye. "its the minor infraction that snowballs."

Now, with apparent knuckle dragging from her police force, and a brief but troubling phone call from those on high, Lucinda had to bow to pressure and make it known that the she was in charge of the matter, put on a show for the press and convince everyone of the preferred outcome that everyone wanted. Which was how she came to be stood, physically, on the Templeton streets outside police headquarters, in blustery autumn weather, that mussed up her hair and promised only worse to come. She was practically face to face with some of the most deprived citizens of the city; people that her office, and herself, had at one time or another failed. This was the worst the job could offer, and she deeply resented that she had been forced into this position. It was essential that she conceal this indignation, however, and Lucinda concentrated on the words she had skimmed over in the back of the car, and tried to relax the muscles in her face to rid it of the scowl that should rightfully be there.

She was surprised how clean South Boulevard

appeared in that afternoons gloom, and took heart from the fact the city's hygiene department was clearly still functioning. As her aides prepared the microphone at the dais, and the crush of reporters and cameramen grew steadily, her eyes roamed the boundaries and barriers her security team had hastily assembled, only about forty minutes previously. She was assured by the very visible presence of police officers, watching on closely and equipped to move in if necessary. At least they had got that right, she thought.

Much to her consternation, her gaze fell on a small cluster of people, near the front of the growing crowd of spectators and on the left of her direct field of vision; all of a fairly youngish age. They were there to attract attention, for a purpose, and being very vocal about it, but it was the image emblazoned on their T-shirts that concerned Lucinda the most. It was a black and white print of the winged man, the one who called himself Icarus, and she had no doubt they were some kind of fan base of this troublesome 'superhero'. She got the attention of her closest bodyguard, and whispered directions over her shoulder. He calmly nodded and brought a radio up to his lips, and within seconds, a couple of the officers on duty had slowly shifted into position, a lot closer to that group. They had to be careful, she realised, because any attention they drew to that part of the crowd, then there was the danger that those T-shirts and those chants may end up on the evening news.

Eager to get this spectacle commenced and ended as soon as possible, Lucinda turned and nodded at her crew, who called for quiet from the assembled press. An approximation of silence descended, and she approached the microphone and waited until she was certain the cameras were rolling, and she had commanded everyone's attention. After thanking everyone for attending, she paused for a beat and looked down at the notes she had arranged and ordered, out of shot.

"I am aware, as I'm sure you're all aware, of some of the challenges and the difficulties we all face in this city," She began. "Life can be tough, and we have all been working hard, as I'm sure you all work hard, to make ends meet and keep our lives on track, and to provide for our homes, and our families. This has to be priority one, for all of us, to keep our homes and our families safe. To have law and order, to have a functioning police force, and to feel safe in our city."

Lucinda looked up then, to make eye contact here and there, for effect, but also because there was a little feedback from the audio equipment that someone from the team was scrambling to fix, and she did not want attention to stray there. "I know there have been setbacks, some bumps along the road," She continued. "There always are, and its right that we should not be satisfied, that we should demand better. Things can always be better, and we can make it better. And we can do that by working together. It is not for any one person, no matter how well intentioned they may be, to take our laws and our order, which we have strived so hard to maintain, to take our safety and our security into their own hands and take control of this city away from the people, away from you."

Lucinda made sure to stress the words that added strength to her speech, to give it the threat and weight she intended. She had attended many hours of training in this regard and knew all too well how necessary it was. Her message had to be clear and sobering.

"I've worked hard for this city, I have family I care about, I care about law and order. I refuse to allow anyone to take this away from us and to undermine our police services, our justice system, the laws and rules of our society that keep us together and keep us safe. It may not be perfect, but its all we have, and we cannot let the deranged ideology of a violent fugitive make us forget that, to throw away what we have taken so long to build. This man that calls himself Icarus, he has a voice, and he has made it heard. But we are a city of many voices, from many backgrounds, and we must try to make room for every voice, to let everyone have their say. We are proud to say we live in a democracy, and I will not stand by and watch while some lone vigilante runs riot through our streets and tries to tell us what is best for society, to impose his vision upon us. That is not what makes our country great, and that is not what a democracy stands for."

On television, the news channels airing the live broadcast were appreciating the audience figures. Ms Watson's speech had been keenly anticipated and the public clearly wanted to hear what she had to say. It was only a few channels, about half way through, that dared interrupt her speech and go to the other broadcast that was breaking live, right at that moment. Icarus was streaming a new announcement, and while many producers elected to run with the governors speech to the end and go back to his recording, the braver ones cut her words short to go directly to the familiar sinister figure, sat in the darkened background. By contrast, his words were not comforting or reassuring, nor were they seeking approval or to appease anyone. Icarus clearly did not care how he came across or the impression he made, and he spoke with a croaky, pressing menace.

"No one now can doubt my sincerity, I think I've

convinced you all of that, and only a fool would underestimate my abilities," Icarus began, behind the formidable helmet and within the fuzziness and hiss of lesser quality picture and audio. "I mean what I say when I tell you I am devoted to hunting down and eliminating the bad and the rotten and the corrupt in our society. I will show no mercy, and this may be the first time in a long time a figure in the public eye has said something to you that is honest, and truthful. Not from me will you hear hollow promises and politically correct lies. Right now, you will be seeing the first signs of their fear, of the establishments nervousness. You will see the police are deployed, you will watch the media stir up outrage, and all the voices you will hear will be telling you how dangerous I am; how it is I who is a threat to your way of life. To your safety."

Here, Icarus leant back for a beat, as if preparing himself, or enjoying himself, in anticipation of what was to come next. He raised a gloved finger in warning.

"Do not listen to their lies. I will not be cowed by their threats. It is not Icarus who must be afraid, it is not I who will back down. There can no mercy, and I will spare no one from my quest to rid this world of their evil. If you have meddled in damaging trade, pillaged resources from lands that don't belong to you, profited from the suffering of others or the poisoning of our environment, you are not safe from me. Your gold and your armies and your power will not keep you safe. The next victim of Icarus will be one of the highest standing, a god among capitalists and corporate manipulators. One who thinks he is the master of our race, who need never answer for his actions and can do whatever he wishes without consequence. Icarus will change that view, and my message will be writ loud and clear from the heights of this city. No one is safe from my justice, no crime will go unpunished. Your wealth and your power will not protect you!"

It was then the live stream was cut out.

On South Boulevard, Lucinda Watson was wrapping up her announcement.

"...we will leave no stone unturned or spare any powers we have at our command. Be assured this man will eventually face justice, true justice, and no fancy costume will protect him."

It was then the loudest of the protesters broke through the boundary railing, and the police rushed in to force the spectators back.

9

Just sitting in a chair. Something Raymond did pretty much every day, whether behind his desk or the wheel of a response car. But when you could not do anything else, for hour after hour, it became quickly very torturous. Ray's lower back was in regular spasms, sending electric jolts of agony up his spine; he could no longer move the fingers of his hands, tied behind him (they felt like nothing but heavy, swollen appendages now) and the more he concentrated on not thinking about the piss he needed to take, the more urgent his bladder seemed to swell and protest. Worst of all was the splitting ache, from the back of his neck and up over to his crown, that was a constant, unrelenting throb. From head to foot, he was a mosaic of pain.

In desperation, Ray tried to recall what he knew of meditation, and using the power of the mind to overcome physical hardship. Had he not read somewhere that a Tibetan monk had lasted all winter, sat in an icy cave with nothing to eat or drink, by simply chanting and channelling his own body heat? Or what about that young child he had discovered that time, in the basement of some crack-house, clinging tenuously to life despite the neglect and unpleasantness that that young life offered?

He screwed his eyes shut and ground at his teeth with the effort. How long had it been now? Ray had no objective way of telling. The room was so naturally dark and squalid, it was hard to tell day from evening, and he was unsure when he had arrived here anyway. Did the pain make time seem to go faster, or slower?

And what of his torturer? If residual guilt had inspired any sympathy for the man to whom this flat belonged, it was rapidly eroding away. He tried to concentrate his mind on the case; Lawrence Lowe, proud father, loving husband, grieving victim… and now a revengeful monster. Was he really a lunatic? The man whom he had spoken to was clearly unstable, clearly disturbed, but not quite raving mad. It was possible that the danger that his alter ego, this 'Icarus', presented appeared to Ray to have not yet been fully realised.

Could the two be separated? This was a more problematic question, far beyond Ray's skills and pay grade, but for the sake of his ballooning bladder and stabs of excruciating pain, he considered it regardless. Man from monster; Sense from emotion. Something chimed with Ray right then; Could a man rid himself of pain, separate himself from the tragedy of life, and still remain…a real person? More to the point, was it Ray's place to care any more? If his hands were freed and his gun cocked, loaded and aimed at Lowe's head, would Ray pull the trigger? To end this pain and discomfort, Ray would probably have done anything at all right then, so instead, he reversed the question. Was Lowe/Icarus likely to pull the trigger, on him? How much longer did he have? *If this goes on much longer, I'd fucking beg him to shoot me!*

Suddenly, through the waves of agony, Ray discerned that he was about to learn the answer to this question at least. Footsteps hurried in place behind the front door, ten yards from him, and blinking through the self-imposed, blackening blur of his sight, Ray observed the door smash inward and a dark, suited figure rush inside and toward him, with what looked like a rifle swing up in front of it. Ray could sense the proximity of the cool oval of the steel barrel, levelled neatly an inch or two from his temple, and he gave up trying to bring the world into clarity and let his eyes shut. Finally resigned to his fate, Ray felt his bladder blissfully relax at the same time, as he released the pent up urine into his lap

A gruff, familiar voice then, and one that did anything but fill Ray with relief.

"For fuck's sakes," said Jameson. "Someone untie Knight. And get a fresh pair of pants someone?"

10

Lalonde was in his element, at the head of the squad and with a fixed stare, no doubt imagining and fantasizing about the confrontation to come. With every bump and vibration of the vehicle, Ray felt a remnant of pain shoot up his back and in his wrists. Bandaged, and watered, what remaining dignity he could muster compelled him to insist on going with the team back to Shoremouth, if only to be certain they arrived as quickly as possible at the right warehouse. It had earned him no reprieve from the disgust of Jameson, while Watts remained stony and silent, but nobody objected to him sharing one of the vehicles.

He sat in the back of an SUV with Brooks and two others, and the police Chief sat in the passenger seat with Williams driving. Through the window, and the trickle of rain sliding down the glass, he could see the armoured response vans in front, containing Lalonde and his crew, and the passing vista of Templeton, growing dark once more. The city was slipping into its most natural and comfortable guise of night. They had heard snippets of Icarus's words, and much of the Governor's speech, over the utility vehicles radio, and Ray wondered if the man he had met just that morning, if he was ever going to see him again, alive and fearsome, or on some medical gurney, bloody and lifeless.

The vehicle shook to a halt. They had arrived.

Lalonde kicked open the back doors of the van in front and leapt out, taking up a crouch a short distance away to observe his men decamp and gather in a solid, silent and ready formation. A moment or two to check their armoury, and he was satisfied the regiment were prepared for action. There was an intense pause, when Knight realised they were waiting for his direction, and he slid open the side of the SUV and pointed out the tall sheet metal doors of the next unit down.

"There's a smaller door in the far corner, its not locked."

Lalonde glanced at Jameson, leaning out the passenger window of the second van, who nodded, then he got up from his crouch and quickly moved down the street. His men followed in neat procession, and outside the far doorway, he gave the order to move in.

*

Preparedness, and foreseeing every worst case scenario; he had known all along it would be the only way. There must be nothing that could possibly take him by surprise, or catch him unawares.

Even so, while hefting the device in his palm up to his face, he felt a deep pang of regret for what he was about to do. He had sacrificed so much, and what he had spent so patiently trying to establish was now to be obliterated as well.

Change was constant. Life must be fluid and reactionary; to remain the same was poison. Adapt and survive, kill and move on. He had to remember that. Live and fight again.

*

"Stay back, van two," Howard Watts commanded from the front seat of the passenger van."Radio silence from now."

"Roger that." came the voice of Jameson in reply.

On the back seat, Raymond could not bring himself to look at his boss, but he found a warmth in the expression of his young charge. Carl asked him if he was okay. Ray just shrugged, and they both exchanged a look to silently affirm they suspected the worst was to come.

As if the city wished to corroborate that assessment, the first sounds from within the warehouse emerged.

A dull concussion, and then yelling, and now a strangled shout. Before the first figure began to dash back out onto the street, an enormous tremor seemed to shake the earth beneath them. And then all of a sudden the entire roof of the warehouse erupted into blinding yellow flame, lighting up the city sky. What once had been the hideout of 'superhero' Icarus was now blown a hundred feet up into the air in a tremendous explosion

11

"How's the picture?"

The helicopter turned around for another swoop over the top of the estate, aiming for one building in particular that still had trails of smoke raising from it into the morning sky.

"Weather is so fucking grim its hard to pick out the smoke. Can we increase the contrast?"

"Does that look a little shaky to you? How was that camera mount looking?"

The image relayed over several screens in the studio were stabilized and cropped for broadcast. The head technician signalled they were ready and the babble over the intercoms continued.

"Can we zoom in on the police cars? Can you get that close?"

"Any paramedics, body bags?"

The network helicopter hovered over the remains of the warehouse near the centre of the Shoremouth estate, and the pilot teased the controls to try and satisfy the instructions coming through his earpiece. Toward the corner of the street, a cluster of vans marked the boundary of the press camp, and while reporters there wrestled with their equipment, several police officers stood guard close by to make sure they did not advance any further.

"Are we ready for Angela? Is she ready, David?"

The establishing shots were broadcast and the

news anchors announced the story and provided some background on the breaking news. Several of the screens in the studio switched to Angela Draper, framed in a mid-shot and still adjusting her own earpiece. She nodded at some instruction, waved off a hair stylist, and then her body stiffened as she focussed her gaze into camera. On the count of one, her face brightened suddenly into a wide smile.

"A new chapter has unfolded in the story of Templeton's own Superhero here near the dockyards to the West of the city, as Police, acting on vital new information, attempted last night to storm the secret lair of the controversial figure that calls himself 'Icarus'..."

"That's terrific, Angela."

"Close in on the front of the building, or on the roof. Try and get me some wreckage, will you?"

"Are we ready on the Police reel? When should we cut to the statement?"

"That's it, get closer, Angela. Be great if the officer stops you, don't worry."

Kept closely in shot, the reporter started to move further down the street, toward the area widely fenced off with yellow police tape. "… As far as we understand it, while the premises does seem to be the location of the winged avengers broadcasts, and evidence is still being recovered to confirm this, the raid itself was a failure. No capture of Icarus has been announced, and it is assumed that he made good his escape. We can't yet confirm if he was in the building at the time of the raid, or if he fought his way out and the destruction we see this morning is the aftermath of that encounter. Either way, this comes as great relief to many, including of course his many fans..."

"Great, okay cut away to the crowd shots, David."

In shot now were a dense group of men and women, most of them fairly youthful, cheering and smiling and holding up banners. A couple of them held their arms high to show fabricated wings strung about their shoulders, in imitation of their hero, while others wore imitation Greek helmets over their heads. The yells and messages all seemed to support and declare their love for Icarus, and a steady pan across the mass of people picked out some of the images on their T-shirts, which were freshly printed with various depictions of the winged man. One in particular appeared to portray a man posed against the spread of wings behind him, in a fashion very similar to Christ on the cross.

This last made Howard Watts raise his remote in despair and pause the action on the big screen set up in the headquarters task room. Even Jameson, watching over his shoulder, went silent, as Watts shook his head in weary wonder.

"They see him as some kind of god damn Christ figure, now!"

As much to change the topic, Jameson asked, "What shall we do with Icarus's identity? You know any breakthrough we can release to the press will look like a win for us."

In one swift movement, The chief of Police slid the palm of his hand down the length of his face, as if to erase the stress and distaste that had bedded in there from the news bulletin. He considered the question for a moment before looking at his operation head and shrugging slightly.

"I say we bury it for now. God forbid we get a bunch of copycat super hero wannabe's, then how else we gonna tell the wacko's apart? Shit, Tom, we can't look much worse in the public's eye right now..."

Jameson nodded. "And Knight?"

At this, Watts let out a long, ominous sigh. "Let me deal with Knight. That dipshit has been on the force nearly as long as I have."

*

This time, Raymond Knight knew there was only going to be one outcome. There would be no bluffing his way out of it, nor any use in standing his ground. He had deviated from protocol and jeopardized a high profile operation, and there were few things worse an officer could do in law enforcement. In short, he had screwed up. Badly. He did not have the seniority nor the connections to slip his way out of the inevitable consequences, not some jobbing lowlife like him, and the bruises, black eye and his general pathetic appearance would win him no sympathy

He raised his hand and knocked on his Captain's door. A loud bark came from the other side, which Ray understood to mean 'come in', but before he did, he slid a hand inside his jacket pocket and popped a toothpick into his mouth.

Howard, talking into a phone receiver as always, motioned Ray to come in and take a seat. There were only two, comfortable 'tub' chairs, aside from the Chief's large desk, by way of furniture in the office. The rest of the space was taken up by shelves of filing and filing cabinets, a water dispenser and a tall, conspicuous house plant beside the window at the back. Ray took one of the tub seats at a safe distance from the desk, gnawing furiously on the splinter of wood in the corner of his mouth.

Howard Watts concluded his phone call and sat back, staring at his lieutenant and smoothing down the remains of his hairline at the back of his head. If his blank features appeared to be weighing anything up right then, it was clear he had made a decision when he sighed and folded his arms across his chest. “Raymond, I won’t sit here and try feed you some B.S. We both know you what you did was unacceptable and, well, it couldn’t have been at a worse possible time. You were already on thin ice, and you just went smashing on through. I don’t wanna flap around going into the ins and outs of it all and take statements, I think we’re both experienced enough to realise what you did just can’t slide, is that fair to say?” Watts raised a hand, palm upward, inviting a response, but Ray just nodded. This seemed to satisfy the older man, although a wince of discomfort seemed to make him hesitate.

“We’ve worked together in this place for some time now and it pains me to have to bring you in here and tell you what I have to say, truly it does, but, anyway, it is what it is.” There was an awkward pause after this, before Watts added, “Is there anything you wish to say, Raymond? For the record?”

Ray looked down at his feet and his brow screwed up tight. He had a million things to say, but he could not work out which things needed saying most urgently, nor how to express them so they made any sense.

“Go easy on the Kid, Brooks, as a last favour to me, will you? He’s a good one, you could use him.” That much was easy enough for him to say, he knew it was true and he meant it, but what he felt compelled to offer next had to be forced out. “Look, Howie, I know you got your job to do, and I know it ain’t easy, but...When you get this guy, Chief, this 'Icarus', go easy on him, will you?" Ray met his soon-to-be-ex boss's eyes, he hoped with the same force of will he felt. "He...He's not a bad guy, not all the way through, I know. He's been turned into one. I thought...If I could have had another hour or two with him, maybe..." Rays voice trailed off along with any conviction he had left.

Watts regarded his lieutenant for a moment more, then waved his hand in front of him to indicate he had heard enough. He leant forward in his chair and started to adjust and fuss over the papers on his desk, perhaps thinking about something, perhaps trying not to think about anything. When he looked back up at his soon-to-be-ex detective again, it was with a sour expression that was mirrored in the long, slow sigh that accompanied it. His big balding head sank into his shoulders.

"Time for negotiation with this guy has long since passed, Ray, and I don't wanna hear what you think about it. If he was in custody now, after we had busted his hideout, then, maybe, but as it stands...I have to put you on suspension, as of today. Maybe when this shit storm dies down we can do something about saving your pension, but for now...I have to ask you to leave this department. Clear your desk and report to HR with your I.D. and firearm. Don't come into work tomorrow, someone will call you and work out where we take it from here. I'm sorry, Raymond."

*

Nothing left.

No drones, no isolation tanks, no gym, no computer bank, no hardware. Almost all of his supplies and equipment had gone up in smoke and he was left with nothing but the garage he stood in, a laptop and few trunks and suitcases. He had already done an inventory on its contents, and it did not make for encouraging news.

A small parcel of plastic explosive, a taser, some sprays, a single, ultralight nylon parachute and a few spare clothes, hardly enough to launch the revolution he had promised. Worse still, the funds in the bank account were at their limit, and he could not foresee another deposit for at least two weeks. The rent on this garage was overdue on top of everything else.

He had invested in the double garage, situated behind of one of the more remote suburbs of the city, shortly after he had taken the little grubby room down town. He thought he may one day need an emergency back up, to hole up and replenish stores, and the monthly rental was negligible. He had put in a big freezer, a small cot bed and installed a sink and toilet, but the walls were only bare breeze block and the roof little more than corrugated metal sheeting. Basic and practical, he had not intended on living here for more than a couple of days, at the most, but now, he could see no option but to call it home.

If he could just do this one last mission, pull it off even in a more modest, less spectacular fashion, perhaps then he could afford to lay low for a while? Just escape in the van and take off, cross a border and recoup. Already, he had observed online some of the first signs of imitators, people taking on the baton and beginning to stand up for themselves. His message of intolerance was spreading and catching on, He could not afford to let it falter now.

12

A parched desert plain, barren and sweltering under a relentless sun. A young girl, clothed in nothing but tattered rags, balances a ridiculous load on her shoulders, suspended from a crude wooden pole. Her placid face betrays no suffering, as she traverses a rough dirt road, that seems to lead to nowhere. A family emerges from a patchwork hovel in the thickets beside the path, to greet her and share in the bounty that she has carried to them. The young girl is not alone, as many children of a similar age follow in her footsteps. It is a regrettable but nonetheless moving scene, suddenly interrupted by a helicopter, swooping overhead, and a fleet of trucks, roaring in its wake. The landscape morphs into a vista of modern comfort, with engineers and foremen, busily referring to blueprints and pointing out where the next construction must commence. Now, the girl we saw in rags, is clothed in a regular school uniform, carrying only a shoulder satchel to hold her textbooks, and her face is beaming with a wide grin.

As the commercial ends, the legend emblazoned on screen reads: "Fairmount - Invested in you, invested in the Future!" A silence followed the final swell of the theme music, and everyone in the conference room of floor fifteen waited anxiously for the judgement to arrive. The long teak table had more than a dozen people sat around its curve, but at the centre, given suitable space for his status, the CEO looked on thoughtfully.

Miles Fairmount lowered the hand concealing his

mouth, raised his brows and leant back in his chair, regarding the staff that were hungrily scanning his body language for some kind of approval, appraisal, or any giveaway at all. Eventually, Miles picked up the sheet of figures presented in attractive graphics in front of him, pursed his lips and, without looking up, languidly asked a question of his press secretary. She sat stiffly upright, conscious of the envy around her of being consulted first.

"Yes, Mr Fairmount. We have secured air time on the major news channels and a slot during the COP31 conference. We can be fully represented at the delegation there next month."

And to his project manager, "We had any trouble with the land contracts?"

A man toward the centre of the long table spoke up gingerly, remarking on some matters of relocation and appeasement of local officials. Nothing unexpected or over budget, he was quick to stress.

Miles nodded. "Okay," he said after several moments more inspecting the papers. "I'm ready to go with this." A billion dollar decision, but one he was used to making now. With power and success came a feeling of invulnerability, which he was wary to guard against, but nonetheless, it felt good.

A buzz from the intercom wired into the head of the table interrupted the mood, and his P.A. apologised for interrupting.

"Its Davis, sir, of Security. He said he needs to know what kind of time the entourage should prepare for. He said to remind you its red alert, city wide, tonight."

Damn that fool super hero nonsense, Miles Fairmount thought. How could some nutjob nobody have a bearing on his business? He made little effort to disguise the impatience from his voice when he replied.

"Tell him to put his feet up. I shan't be done here till seven at the earliest."

*

In the lobby of the Fairmount building, the doorman looked through the screen glass doorways at the figure waiting expectantly on the other side, dwarfed by the height and scale of the glazed facade. His place of repose, always visible, was beside the Fairmount logo, a construction which stood as tall as himself and employed a water-flow effect to cascade over the giant letters, and occupied the centre of the lobby area. He was loathe to leave this spot, but after a second tap on the glass screen, he grudgingly crossed the granite-slab tiled floor and admitted the bemused looking figure.

The man was in overalls and carried a shoulder bag and clip board, and introduced himself as Paul Manning, the Fire Safety Risk Assessor. The mature doorman was neither impressed nor moved by the letter headed paper on his clipboard or the company name branded on the back of the overall. A quizzical frown about the doorman's brow prompted the visitor to explain further. "All your stair wells and common areas have extinguishers and alarms on every floor. These need to be tested as working and made sure they're not out of date every six months. It's gonna take me the next couple of days at least, but only if I get started now." acknowledging the emphasis on '... now...', but refusing to be harried, the doorman gestured for the man to wait and quietly radioed in to security.

"Hey,Phil. Gotta health and safety type at the front desk here, something about Fire Risk Assessment. We book anything in like that?" While talking, the doorman discretely scanned the visitor, from top to bottom. Late middle age, spoke with a local accent, had the build for physical, active work. "Check that, will do."

The conversation ended, the doorman asked to see inside the shoulder pack. The visitor duly obliged, swung the bag to the floor and unzipped he top. The doorman was reluctant to crease his immaculate long black jacket leaning down, and was grateful when the man picked through some of the equipment and explained their uses. 'Live wire detector', 'Battery tester', 'Sensor Sounders', 'Insulation cable' were some of the items, all attributed to suitably anonymous looking gadgets and contraptions. The man spoke in an offhand way, with a combination of impatience and boredom that the doormen knew well from past encounters with trades people and builder types. Eventually, the doorman nodded and led the man to the reception desk.

"Book him in please, Jackie," This to the glamorous but quietly austere young lady behind the desk, before turning back to the Fire Risk Assessor. "Please wear your visitor pass at all time and stick only to the common areas."

The visitor accepted his pass, nodded gratefully at the doorman and receptionist in turn, then paced forward past the luxurious settees and ornate oak dividers that graced the rest of the lobby area. Lawrence Lowe had successfully infiltrated the Fairmount building, and part two of his plan could commence.

13

Despite the warnings from the major news channels earlier that day, Templeton had if anything come more alive and active with the approach of night and showed no signs of slowing. Traffic and lights swarmed into the centre, while people and noise filled the streets with the anticipation of an event that nobody could define. It was a tantalizing mystery, and certainly nobody cared if the event were enlightening or catastrophic. There was just a palpable sense everywhere that something seismic was about to occur that night, and many of the people of Templeton did not want to miss it.

Nor too did the police. Along with the full roster of patrol cars in service, several armoured vehicles rolled slowly into place at strategic stations around the major landmarks and corporate strongholds, in the financial and trading districts, while at least one track mounted missile launcher had arrived on loan from the closest military defence base. The city was plainly on full alert, but the police presence did nothing to dilute the near-carnival atmosphere that infected the air as night took a hold and the neon and spotlights started to illuminate the streets.

Angela Draper took great pains to describe the feeling as she too cruised the roads in a network van, remarking on the number of people and the passing police cars. At intervals, they would stop and quiz an excitable group of night crawlers, and ask them how they felt and what they were doing.

“This is payback, man,” One clearly intoxicated Templeton resident was eager to comment. “He’s got the elite running scared, man. Look around, you can see how scared they are with the hardware they got deployed everywhere. Do you see this every night when one of us are shot or raped or victims of a gangland shooting? No, we do not, but when one of 'Them' is threatened, it's a different story, man. I wouldn't miss this for the world. Payback, man, I hope Icarus takes 'Them' all out, these corrupt, corporate scumbags, the <bleep> a <bleep> hero, man, a genuine, living Super Hero!"

*

Right then, Lawrence Lowe was unpacking the costume and preparing to "transform". He had not had the time or means to rescue the full suit and body armour that had fairly successfully shielded his body up to now, although several tightly bandaged wounds and fractured bones were evidence otherwise. All that he had been able to salvage was a slimmed-down version of the suit and a fibreglass coated chest plate. Skateboarding pads had to protect his elbows and knees now, and the helmet was no longer steel reinforced. Instead, he slipped over his head a covering like a balaclava which he had sewed around a wire mesh. The interlocking plated wings were now no more than a rubberised cloak, attached around his neck.

An hour earlier he had ventured onto the corridor servicing two giant office floors of traders and fund managers. They were so busy schmoozing and haggling that they barely glanced in his direction, He had strayed there to look out over the city and count the helicopters circling above. A stressed looking suit paused to join him at one moment, and he took the opportunity to test his resolve

"You think they're police, hunting down that fella Icarus?"

The young man shook his head vigorously and pointed. "No. You see that number, nine? That's a news channel, hoping to be first at the sight of any action that kicks off"

Lawrence pushed his luck. "You really think he'll strike again with all this shit going down?"

A grin. "I believe he's just crazy enough to go through with it, why I like him. Security has us all on a high terror alert this evening. You know we're a potential target, don't you? what with old man Fairmount being in the Bildenburg crowd."

Lawrence feigned his ignorance, until the suit got bored and rejoined the boiler room, and he returned to the stairwell. Since then he had been laying low on the eigth floor watching on a screen the relay from his last micro drone he had landed on an adjacent roof. By adjusting the focus of the lens and cropping the image on his tablet, he had been able to observe the people attending the meeting on the fifteenth floor, taking place behind enormous walls of glass which were conveniently well lit. He was certain Fairmount was sat at the head of the long table in there, and by seven thirty that evening, nearly all of the participants had exited the room. The big man remained.

Having left the clipboard behind, he had swung the holdall into the nearest lavatory and unpacked the suit from the false bottom. Stripped of the fire safety coveralls, he had carefully changed and removed from the bag all the instruments and devices that he planned on deploying.

The small can of kerosene, the plastic explosive and detonators, the personal tazer and dart-loaded pistol all fit into the tool belt around his waste, while the length of cable was looped behind. The flash bomb he considered leaving behind, but at the last moment, opted to hoop into the belt as well. This done, he emptied the quarter litre bottle of electrolyte fluid mixed with a mild amphetamine solution, four ten milligram tablets of annabol and a crushed sodium morphate as a painkiller. He did not care about the acrid taste. Wasting no further time, he ran up to the fifteenth floor and opened the fire escape door, remaining briefly the other side of it, his ear pressed close to the opening. Satisfied there was no one in the corridor, he ducked in and silently advanced up the hallway.

To their equal surprise, a young woman emerged from behind a rest room door just as Lawrence reached it. He halted abruptly and she gasped, holding a hand over her mouth and staring at him from head to foot.

"A Surprise, for the old man's birthday," Gesturing at his costume. "Thought it would be funny."

She allowed a flicker of a smile, but studied him closer still. "Yeah, funny. But I didn't think his birthday was till August."

Even before she had finished the sentence, Lawrence had slipped the dart gun from the holster, and with a twist of his wrist, shot her from his hip so the tiny dart landed home just above her left breast. She gave a shrill squeal, and looked down at the mini projectile and the tiny speck of blood that was growing around it. A second later, she backed into the toilet again, shaking her head from side to side and murmuring incoherently. Lawrence followed her in, his left hand raised placatingly as he repeated "it's okay" gently and soothingly. Her eyes widened as she stumbled back against the toilet wall, and suddenly her mouth opened and she began to let out a terrified scream. In an instant, Lawrence stepped beside her and swung her around so he could clasp her hands by her sides and enclose her mouth with a gloved hand at the same time.

A minute passed, while her body spasmed and convulsed against him, and he tried not to look at her eyes, rolling around in her head in abject terror. Another minute, and the Rohypnol took effect, her convulsions eased and her body relaxed. Her eyelids fluttered to a close and he manoeuvred her into a cubicle and set her down on the toilet seat.

At the end of the corridor, the main suite, and he wasted no time flinging open the door and advancing inside. The surprise on the man's face was evident, but fleeting, as his high stakes composure returned to him swiftly and he reached under his desk with his right hand. Lawrence raised the gun and pulled the trigger again, this time the dart hitting home just below Fairmount's collar bone.

Springing over his desk, he pushed the man back against the wall. Fairly spry, given his well funded training and medical regime, the old man resisted with substantial ferocity. Lawrence took out his knees with a low kick, and moved in quickly for a head lock, his arm reaching around his throat and holding him there, on his knees, until the Rohypnol took effect.

With the cable, he hog tied his hands and ankles, looped one end over the light fixture and hauled the dead weight into the air. Lawrence then aimed the kerosene nozzle at the wall and sprayed the fluid in a pattern he had practised twice before, that of a dollar sign. He then prodded the plastic explosive in several areas around the sill of one of the main great windows, pushed in two detonators, and unravelled the wire for several metres. He pushed over a tall cabinet, hunkered down behind it and depressed the switch. With a startling eruption, the glass blew in all directions while the plaster around the wall formed a pale dust cloud, that the night sucked out through the new opening.

Igniting the kerosene, so a fierce yellow flame formed the sign of the dollar, Lawrence stepped up to the edge of the window and remained there, the damning symbol burning behind him. He did not want to move until he saw the helicopters turn in his direction. A second, two, then he saw over the pinnacles and turrets of the cityscape a searchlight revolve in the sky and angle toward his direction. He observed, too, the pause in traffic directly below, in the streets two hundred, three hundred feet down, as the sound of sirens came to him from approaching police cars.

They were coming, but he would not end this act until it was made clear that he had done it. The search light swept over the shattered window on the fifteenth floor, and Icarus stood firm as the beam picked out his outline. He raised his arms, and let the cloak spread out either side of him. He could hear the heavy beat of the choppers blades as it approached, holding the pose a second more.

Now, he was running. Back down the corridor, through the fire escape, and back onto the stairwell. His momentum took him onward, three steps at a time, as he raced down from one floor to the next. He counted the numbers he glimpsed as he passed them. Floor nine, eight, seven. He got to floor four before he heard the sounds of footsteps coming up from beneath, as troopers came up the stairway to intercept him. Immediately, Lawrence pushed open the nearest door and entered the fourth storey.

The far end of the office space overlooked the

company car park, and gripping the edge of one of the windows there, he pulled it backward and leant out over the drop below.

In the rush of air, he searched beneath him until his eyes lighted on a distribution lorry, parked twenty yards from the side of the building, taking up several bays of the park. He calculated the distance and trajectory, then launched himself out of the window and into the night air.

He fell thirty feet, or about two storeys, his arms suspended above him to slow his fall. A second later and he impacted onto the roof of the lorry trailer and rolled off and down the remaining ten feet to the ground. As soon as his knees crumpled under him, Lawrence felt something give in his knee cap, and he tried to twist onto his side to take some of the force of the landing away from his legs.

As he righted himself, he was only able to stagger at speed down the parking ramp and out of the buildings rear and onto an adjoining street. Here, amid the growing sounds of helicopter engines and sirens, he noticed a police car pull up at the corner, and the two officers inside climbed out of the vehicle and started talking into a radio.

Lawrence flattened himself against the wall, and staying as still as he possibly could, he tried to get his breathing under control. His eyes never left the policemen, which was how the four inebriated men took him by surprise. They hushed when they saw him, but as soon as his costume registered, they began to holler and exclaim excitedly.

"Hey!" "It's him!"

Glancing round, Lawrence saw that the officers were looking in their direction, and then they re-entered the car and started to manoeuvre it around. Lawrence pushed past the men, and took off at a hobbling jog down the next alley behind them.

The walkway became so narrow, that the police vehicle could not enter. It pulled up beside a skip, blocking that end of the avenue, and the officers exited the car once more, bringing with them what appeared to be a pump action shotgun. Lawrence waited ahead in a thick pool of dark shadow, motionless, until the officers were within range, then he flicked the switch on the flash bomb and tossed it in front of him. An instant supernova blossomed inside the alleyway, and in those few seconds, Lawrence dived around the corner and scrambled under a familiar looking concrete underpass. He leapt over a railing and tumbled into the freezing waters of the Dunster, letting the strong current of the river sweep him down stream.

14

Optics were awoken and they transmitted their light signals into the screens and monitors cabled into the central network of the city. Like an inner eye, the digital interface blinked open and showed the people of the city what it saw. In every apartment, on every office floor and in every shop window, in high definition and on widescreen format, images and recordings of what had happened, what was happening and visuals of what could happen were being transmitted to every eye and ear in range.

Plummeting graphics depicted stocks and shares sliding into uncertain limbo, and business gurus shook their heads in woeful consternation. Numbers indicated that prices in supermarkets could become suddenly higher and life for the public in general, announced the grave looking news anchors, was about to take a downturn.

And on that mornings breaking exclusive, Lucinda Watson appeared once more before an army of microphones and her voice became echoed across a half million bandwidths.

“I have just attended an emergency meeting with the ministry of defence, and they assure me that they will be lending any assistance, military or otherwise, that our police forces require to bring this reign of domestic terrorism to an end. I have every confidence that the combined forces of this city’s police department can apprehend this criminal and bring him to justice. And I mean proper justice, not the violent, destructive street justice this man claims to uphold."

It was a defiant announcement; almost a declaration of war, and every television but one was tuned into the Governor right then. Raymond Knight had no interest in what the woman had to say, or how the manhunt was going, or how the market was reacting. He did not wish to hear anything about the winged superhero, good or bad. In fact, he wished that he did not have to hear about him ever again, and angrily stabbing at the buttons, flicking through the channels, he finally hit the mute button and tossed the remote across the sofa.

He shuffled into his bathroom, cupped his hands under the tap, and splashed the water into his face. He did this three, four times before he was willing to straighten up and look back at the face in the mirror there. It did not make for pleasant viewing. The angry bruise that had swollen most his left cheek and eye, from his fight with Icarus, had dulled into a general darkening of that socket. The split lip was still sore, and the bridge of his nose was still tender.

His mood and all round outlook on life was as gruesome as his appearance. In the last month and a half he had been shot at, beaten, kidnapped, forced to discharge a firearm, and kicked off of the force. He had basically had his worst fears scooped out of his mind and smeared into his face. Worse still, he had not done any workouts for two whole days, he felt terrible, and from a confirmatory glance at the crumpled packets and ashy mess on the coffee table, he had started smoking again.

He flopped back down onto the sofa, and for the umpteenth time contemplated how his life could have come undone so completely, and what he could ever do about it. He wanted to call his wife, to speak to Catherine, more than anything, but he would not dial the number. Instead, he plucked another cigarette out from the pack and let it hang from the side of his mouth while he retrieved the television remote. He had little hope of finding consolation from the widescreen, but he could not think of anything else to do. For a moment at least, he found the bright, colourful characters of an old cartoon serial somewhat distracting.

It had to be a Fleisher, or early Ralph Bakshi creation, and it depicted a man in bright blue spandex, zooming through the skies. There was seemingly no escape from Knight's purgatory, it seemed, but it was surprisingly well animated, for the age of the piece. The hero carried the villain by the scruff of his lapel, and deposited him neatly outside the city police station. When the policeman emerged, he looked in wonder at the flying man, and then shared an affectionate salute with the hero. At this, Ray leant forward out of his chair, suddenly gripped. He let the cigarette fall from his mouth, and froze in wide eyed wonder as the credits signalled the end of the cartoon.

He did not wait for the next cartoon to begin, but flicked off the television and reached for his cell phone.

*

"I could get fired just being seen with you!"

Carl Brooks did not appear particularly excited about reuniting with his ex partner, but Knight had done anything he could, including playing on his sympathies, to persuade him to meet with him that evening. In the end, his insistent, positive tone must have won the younger man over. They stood by the river, on the outskirts of the city, in a stiff, chilly breeze. Ominous rumblings and churning black clouds threatened an approaching storm, and while the detective was wrapped up well in his suit and long coat, Ray was still in his track suit bottoms and pullover. Brooks looked the older man up and down, with open concern.

"How you doing, anyway? You look terrible."

Knight shrugged off the comment. "Thanks, but listen to me Carl. Our man, he thinks he's a superhero, right? Well, why don't we try treating him like one. How many superheroes can you think of that make an enemy of the police? They don't, they always work together, in partnership. They're supposed to help each other out, right?"

If Ray's voice and words sounded manic, his alarming appearance did nothing to dilute this impression. If he was having some kind of a nervous breakdown, Carl was even less inclined to humour him and tempted instead to call for help. But, he was still uncertain just how well he knew this man; what kind of well of inner reserves and experience he may be able to draw upon. He was uncertain enough to continue listening.

"We could use this, Carl. Tap into it, and reach out to Icarus instead of chasing him down rabbit holes. We could be able to lure him out, and bring him to us," Ray was clearly getting exasperated trying to get across what he had in mind. "think of the public opinion right now; we can't just hunt this man down and shoot him dead like some wild, rabid dog! They won't swallow it, it'll cause chaos, riots in the streets! We have to try something else, try something a little more...I don't know..."

His voice trailed off, and his head began to drop, but Carl Brooks was silent as he regarded his ex partner. In the end, he said softly, "So, what are you thinking?"

15

Lawrence lay on the mattress, arms and legs splayed, his eyes closed, just concentrating on breathing. For all intents and purposes he looked nothing more than a stick man, like the crude figure depicted in his calling card. Still, and quiet. Except, there was nothing hopeful about the image now, and in the gloomy, damp confines of the back street garage, the man was barely clinging to life.

Every four or five minutes, he would convulse into motion with a racking series of explosive sneezes, which would gradually subside into a miserable lament of sniffing and snuffling. And then he would lie still again, trying to breathe. Trying not to think about the pain.

The bullet wound in his shoulder had failed to heal properly, and now stiffened his entire arm. All he felt was an odd pin-prick tingling, up and down the limb, and it worried him. The ligament damage in his knee combined with a suspected broken toe (it had swollen to twice its normal size) made walking an ordeal, and the cracking at his ribs made breathing no less arduous. It was the cut over his hip that concerned him most, however. It had been deep enough to require a couple of stitches, but the hour he had spent thrashing about in the oily waters of the Dunster had not helped at all. If a bacterial infection were to spread throughout his system now, that would be game over. He had almost exhausted his entire supply of Iodine washing out his various cuts and grazes, and now all he could do was lie still and let his internal biology get on with it.

Without any physical training to activate and focus

the steroid supplements, the tablets just made him feel queasy, and the anti inflammatories he took were not sitting well with his stomach. He had been eating out of cans and jars for the last three days, and the powdered nutrient shakes were running low. Added to this, the worsening cold and damp was almost impossible to control in this dank and poorly insulated enclosure. All he had was a single two-bar convector heater which he kept by his side constantly, and a camping bag he hugged close about him to keep warm.

There was nothing he could do except listen to the steady drip of rain water falling from the exposed beams above, and maintain the routine of sleeping and resting and taking the tablets and more resting. Just lie still, keep warm and wait. And pray, for recovery.

*

"I could shoot you dead where you stand, Knight, and I'd get off with it. What the fuck are you thinking Carl? You that desperate to join your partner on unemployment?"

Howard Watts stood in his office, which Ray had only left in disgrace four days previously, regarding the two men before him with little short of contempt, while behind them, Tom Jameson watched on with his arms crossed over his chest and a face like a health and safety officer inspecting an old, neglected public toilet in a bad part of town.

"Hear him out, Chief, please," Carl pleaded, his voice sounding small. "I think its only fair. I wouldn't be here if I didn't think it was worth it, and, really, what have we got to lose?"

Watts narrowed his eyes and raised his chin, trying to weigh up the risk of listening to these two madmen or having them shot dead. Under the glare, Raymond suddenly felt keenly aware of the absurdity of what he was proposing, and he shifted nervously from one foot to the other. In the end, the Chief of police forced himself to repose against the side of his desk and recapture some kind of calm and composure. The threat in his voice was no less intimidating, as he addressed Ray directly and picked up a porcelain mug, waving it in his direction.

"You got the time it takes me to prepare a fresh cup of coffee, Knight, you better make it good."

*

Five minutes later, the phone in the Chief's Office rang. It was Lucinda Watson, and the look on Watt's face hushed everyone instantly. Few of the people gathered there had ever seen the man try to be polite and courteous to anyone before, but they were witness to the fact right then.

"Yes, Ms Watson, I am serious. This guy has the media wrapped round his little finger and it seems to work in his favour. I don't see why..."

If the Governor's voice had been raised in anger or incredulity, no one in the room could hear it, and the Chief's face gave away nothing. He hummed and made some affirmative noises, then, "Yes, I agree, it will take some co-ordination and there are risks, of course, but you did say, if I recall correctly 'whatever it takes', did you not."

Everyone collectively held their breath. That last comment sounded to all in the room like Watts had drawn a line in the ground and had stepped up to play, and play hard. This was either going to win the day, or bring everything crashing down on top of them. What Lucinda Watson said next, however, made Watts breathe a little easier again.

"You sure about this? Well, I guess it's just about crazy enough to sync in with all the other madness going on right now." There was a moments pause, which Watts guessed was her trying to imagine all the likely outcomes, good and bad, and what they could mean for her. Then she came back, with the decision apparently made. "Fight crazy with crazy, why not? You realise, of course, if all this sinks, Watts, there won't be any coming back? not for you. All right then, so long as we have that clear. What will you need?"

Another few minutes later, and Howard Watts lowered the phone receiver and stared at the small assemblage in his office. No one spoke.

"Well, Raymond," Watts said eventually. "Looks like this whole operation, and this entire police department, sinks or swims on your say so. If you're wrong..." And he left the sentence hanging there.

16

As the end of October approached, the rains intensified. Cascades of water angled down in between Templeton's high rises and towers, drenching everyone unfortunate enough to be outside. It gathered in large pools alongside the pavement, so that passing vehicles sent up freezing waves of rainwater in their wake, and it gurgled up through the overloaded and inadequate drains. It had started to come down thick and heavy the night before, and looked no closer to ending by that afternoon.

It was especially bad on highway two, where the traffic kicked up more of the water from the tarmac, and overworked windscreen wipers did little to improve visibility. Officer Perkins peered over the steering wheel, squinting intently at the brake lights of the vehicle in front, while keeping mindful of the lorry ahead that looked like it was preparing to change lanes. Why had they insisted on the transfer today in the first place? He thought, in between general cursing and swearing at his immediate superiors.

Perkins was a guard at Templeton district prison, and was looking forward to clocking off at midday, when he was awarded the move to the county facility fifty miles away. He had clearly vocalised his objections, and also questioned the timing and urgency of the surprise transfer, but to no avail. In the end, he equated it all to his own bad luck, as, instead of putting his feet up with a cup of coffee and tuning in to the third day of the golf tournament, he was now crawling over the main Dunster bridge, barely doing twenty, in a minimum security transport full of some of the most hardened criminals in the North West. And now, to top it off, the traffic was slowing to a stop in what promised to be an almighty jam.

Perkins swore out loud this time, several times, and through the watery haze, could just make out ahead the lights of a patrol car, likely in the midst of managing a spin out. Quite how this afternoon could get any worse, he did not have the capacity to imagine.

In the back, handcuffed to their ankles on benches along either side, two rows of inmates faced each other and took turns looking out the back window as the van came to a halt. One of the men was so tall and so casually sat, with his knees wide, that the other two on the bench had to angle their bodies away to accommodate him. This clearly angered the inmate opposite, who glared at the taller man with open contempt. He was a bulky, middle aged man whose shaven head seemed to accentuate the grisly aspect of his features, which were currently radiating hate. When he caught the eye of the taller man, he spoke up, rasping the words from between clenched teeth.

"What are you fucking looking at?"

The tall man's face remained placid and composed. The only reaction the words triggered was a slight rise at the corners of his mouth, as if he were about to smile.

"Well? You're such a big man back at Templeton, think you're king of the yard! Well, you wait till we get to the county lock-up, see how tough you are then, you fucking drug peddler!"

The challenge was plain, and everyone in the

vehicle could feel the hate filling up the cramped, uncomfortable space. The two men either side of the taller one, glanced furtively up into the face of the man beside them, watching to see if the words would provoke any kind of reaction or response. Instead, a thick silence was all that followed, while the tall man just continued to smile into the face of the skinhead, their eyes locked in unbreakable contact.

In the cabin, Officer Perkins was inching closer to the source of the grid lock, and the patrol cars filling up both of the lanes up ahead. His gaze was drawn from the scene to his rear-view mirrors, where movement from the traffic behind caught his attention. As he watched, a motorbike was advancing between the rows of vehicles and nearing the transport. Perkins would not have thought twice about it, but when he looked into the other rear mirror, he noticed a second motor cycle doing exactly the same thing. The two bikes drew level with the transport, and as the guard looked out of his side window, he could see the motorbike was ridden by a man in a black helmet and leathers, who brought the bike to a halt and unzipped his jacket. From within, the cyclist withdrew a long, metallic object and swung it in his hands until it was pointed into the cabin of the transport, and directly at officer Perkins head. It took him a second or two before he realised he was looking at a shotgun.

There followed an enormous roar of twin barrels discharging, but this came from the back of the transport. The second biker had blasted the lock at the double doors on the rear of the vehicle, and swinging the doors open, ducked inside. In horror, Perkins considered doing several things all at once, namely, ducking below the dash out of sight of the gun-toting biker, opening the door and running for it, or snatching up the radio and calling for assistance. The biker covering the guard must have sensed his increasing panic, as the helmet just slowly revolved from side to side in a clear gesture of advice. 'Don't.'

Behind him, the second biker had unlocked the tall man's cuffs, dropped something into his lap, and given the key to his companions to free themselves, before returning to the motorcycle and revving the engine loudly. The freed inmates smiled jubilantly and congratulated each other for their luck. "You were right, Trent. We are getting out!"

The tall man said nothing, simply got up from the bench and took the handcuff keys, moving to lower his face over the one inmate still locked in place. Trent Meadows stared coldly into the trembling skinheads wide eyes, savouring the terror that now resided within them. Then he leant back, raised the nine millimetre pistol and shot it once into the inmates neck.

This time, Trent Meadows laughed aloud, before exclaiming in a sing-song voice, "You done! Son,..." all while watching the stricken inmates body jerk and kick out in violent convulsions as he died.

The biker in front returned the shotgun into his jacket, and retrieved instead a small can. This, he shook around the top of the transports cabin and down the vehicles sides, before mounting his motorcycle once more and calmly waiting as one of the inmates took up place on the seat behind him. Before the two motorcycles sped away, one of the drivers tossed something onto the bonnet of the prison van. Perkins watched in renewed horror as, despite the falling rain, the fluid ignited and his view of the outside world was quickly replaced with a fiery inferno.

From the end of the bridge ahead, neither of the two police patrol cars made any attempt to move or intercept the escaping prisoners, nor assist with the burning transport van. Instead, one of the officers brought a radio to his mouth, and started to relay something that no one else could hear over the steady, endless rainfall.

17

Angela Draper was not quite at her glamorous best on that evenings broadcast, but she was none the less emphatic in her delivery of the breaking story from under the wide umbrella, shielding her from the worst of what the city was throwing down. She courageously tipped up one end to indicate the big concrete bridge, framed in the background behind her.

"Reports indicate the suspects made their escape by motorcycle, leaving one man dead at the scene, apparently by gun shot wound. The police department confirm that one of the five men now at large in Templeton city is in fact Trent Meadows, brother of the gangland leader killed earlier last month in that spectacular showdown with Icarus, the city's winged avenger. It would only be speculation at this stage, Brian, but I think there's a good chance this dangerous fugitive may have revenge on his mind and will likely be seeking some confrontation with Templeton's masked superhero,"

As if on cue, another dramatic roll of thunder from the dark skies above made Draper pause. The camera closed in on her face, which was now a mask of seriousness.

"Earlier this evening, Governor Lucinda Watson responded to the press on this troubling new development."

Standing firm and defiant as ever, clearly from the inside of a building, that woman now stood before a microphone and spoke with a grave severity that eclipsed that of the young reporter.

"I can assure you all today, that every action will be taken to secure this city and bring order back to Templeton's streets. Every option available to us will be deployed, and in some cases, that may mean some changes. If there was ever any doubt over how we handled the Icarus crisis, this may now have to wait. Our priorities must be put into perspective, and I think it is clear to everyone that there are more pressing concerns in the city today. Gangland culture and violence are a cancer in our society, and we must not allow it to spread and grow unchecked on our streets. The recapture of Trent Meadows must be our number one goal at this moment, and we must not succumb to any culture of anarchy. I ask you all to respect and get behind our law enforcement offers, and help, not hinder, our attempts to restore peace to this city."

*

Icarus lay on his side, scrolling down pages on his laptop. He had been doing this for several hours now, skimming over words and speed reading for content. He had never really taken time to browse the individual comments beneath his posts, but since he had begun, his concentration had intensified. Millions of likes, tens of thousands of messages of support, of appreciation, of pledged allegiance, of advice, of thanks, of emotion.

So many people, and Icarus had lit a fire under their world, had tipped their lives over into chaos, but their voices had more meaning now, it carried more weight. They may suffer for it. Those in power never gave it up easily, and the authorities had many resources, methods and tactics to bear against them all. The norm was usually to crush dissent, before it took a hold.

There were some in the comments who tried to make the point, to contradict what the others were saying. These voices stood out, and Icarus noticed them. Anonymous, and almost absurdly conservative and middle class, nonetheless their points hit home. What would be the repercussions of some anarchic meltdown?

His campaign so far had been brutally effective, in that he had sown violence and hatred and bloodshed pretty much at will, but now his outcomes, his goals, did not seem so simple, so clear cut. Cold, white fury had driven him this far, and now, on the verge of what Icarus felt might be true change, he had doubts. He doubted himself, and where all his efforts would lead.

Night approached, and dark fell over the dripping gutters and crumbling brick of the garage. Icarus moved to the trunk and retrieved a smallish, rusty and dented lock box, then sat cross legged on the ground holding it in his lap. He lifted the lid, and among the numerous trinkets, photographs and folded papers that were stuffed in there, he picked out a plain sheet of A4 and unfolded it carefully. On the page, in a crude child's crayon, Icarus looked at the image of a figure dressed in sandals, helmet and carrying a sword. At his back, there were long, uneven wings stretching to the edge, and he was reminded of a small boy, fascinated with the myth and legends of ancient Greek stories. Such a wonderful boy, and Icarus let his fingers trace the words scribbled beneath the drawing. 'To dad, love Dominic'.

18

They turned up at the front lobby casually, strolling through the doorways that previously had been bookended by armed doormen. Most everyone there looked in the four peoples direction, but nobody made any comment. They appeared to belong in the building, or at least their manner suggested that, and their smiles, although somewhat sinister, were certainly not out of place in this home of drugs and criminality.

The smiling faces looked upon everyone there, but none of the four paused as they proceeded directly to the elevators. Nobody stopped them; it was nobody's duty to stop them. Every since Shaun Meadows had met his end, the corner plot on Blackbrook estate had descended into decadent neglect. If there was no longer the almost military enforcement presence, then there was now a more chaotic unknown that carried with it an equal, but more random potential for violence. Drug pushers and thieves and curb-crawlers came and went on an hourly basis, all through the day and night, constantly. There was no visitors book, no keys or locks in place, and nobody came to collect any rent. All three floors were a shadowy reflection of life at its most base, with drinking, scheming, sex and needle sharing in every available corner of the property.

The four new arrivals entered the corridor on the third floor to be met with a sonic thrum of heavy bass beats and muted, neon lighting. Bodies sprawled against the walls and swayed in clusters of euphoric indifference. None of this seemed to phase the four, as they continued along the corridor until they entered a series of rooms, knocked through to create a larger area. Here, some of the more sober, larger looking men studied the new arrivals more intensely, whispering warnings to their comrades beside them.

Any party atmosphere or happy vibe was gradually diluted as the presence of the new, unfamiliar people started to resonate and become more apparent. They lingered in the centre of the floor, the fixed smiles and quick eyes taking in all there was to see around them, unhurried, and with no obvious care for the effect their presence was having. Eventually, the taller of the four approached the largest of the rooms on this floor; A grand space with luxury furnishings and fewer inhabitants. The few in this room were already aware that there were uninvited guests among them that evening, and they stood and stared at the man now entering their domain.

Trent Meadows ignored the hostile glares circled around him, and instead scanned the walls and décor as if assessing everything he saw and trying to decide if it was to his taste or not. After several moments, his eyes settled on the man whom he judged to be the most assertive, the most prominent of the inhabitants of this luxurious suite. By this time the background music had been switched off and a distinctly apprehensive silence had fallen over the entire area. Two of the tall man's companions joined him either side of his shoulders, while the last man folded his arms and stood solidly behind them, like a sentry.

The residing authority, a thick-set, shaven-haired man of eastern european origin, and a man of no gentle manner, broke the silence at last.

"What the fuck do you want here?" He barked, bluntly, and defiantly.

Trent Meadows continued to stare and smile for a moment, and then he snorted derisively, before swiftly pulling out a semi automatic pistol and shooting the bald headed man twice in the chest. The big man fell back against the wall, then quickly sank to the floor, clutching at his wounds, his breath coming in short hisses, which now was the only sound to be heard.

"I can do whatever I want, didn't you know? This is MY place now.'

No one there even looked like they were thinking about contending the point, and instead, Trent's three companions filed into the spacious room and sat down, making themselves comfortable, and beginning to study the ladies that were frozen where they stood, with slack-jawed fear.

Trent motioned with the barrel of his gun. "You there can help your friend. Get him outta my sight," two men, after the briefest hesitation, moved swiftly to the bleeding and gasping man, dragging him away with hands under his shoulders.

"And what happened to the fucking music? Like a

god damn funeral in here."

19

Ray looked out over the expanse of the city landscape from the fourth floor window of Police headquarters. His eyes had unfocussed until the busy, individual lights blurred into a seething, colourful mass, while his thoughts bubbled and simmered behind this vision.

He feared and resented this place, cherished and felt protective of this city. He knew all too well the depravity and poison that thrived and infected much of the sprawling structure, but was aware also of the brave struggle and compassion that fought for good on a daily basis. The nurses, the paramedics on their night shifts, the guys running the homeless shelters, the post office counter clerk with a warm smile for the regular customers. The examples of charity and care that kept humanity in check, and, inside himself, Ray questioned his own role in its complex mechanism.

Certainly no 'hero', not by any stretch of the imagination, but, a smaller, quieter voice offered from the back of his mind, *you still turn up for work*. He knocked on the doors and faced up to the bad men. Did that not take some courage?

But then there was the urgent matter at hand, this crisis that had escalated out of all reasonable comprehension. An anomaly, born out of routine procedure, long ago, that was now a giant, ravenous, winged monster, that loomed low over the entire city, choking out all light, and threatening to consume everyone below in its fiery, destructive breath. How had he, in this metropolis of millions, come to be chosen to slay this dragon? Of all the people, why did it have to be him? He had tried for so long not to care, to not get involved. He could easily have stayed on his sofa in his apartment, watching cartoons and eating sugary crap. But yet, here he was.

He finished his coffee and tore his eyes away from the hypnotic miasma outside, turning to search the room for any one who might understand his situation, or listen to him at least; someone like Karen, the one woman who had always wanted to hear about his feelings, and had loved him once for all his weaknesses, regardless. There was no one like that here with him now, and instead, Carl was sat in the corner, fixated on his phone screen, Jameson was busy looking busy, and Watts himself, who was receiving an update from the computer guy, Nick Guyler. If there was anyone here who may have conceivably had previous experience of soul-racking dilemmas, it was his boss. Ray just feared that many years in the hot seat, following orders, may have calcified his heart to any kind of humane compassion.

Ray approached his desk. He had nothing much left to lose right then, so he figured he may as well push his luck as far as he could, until it snapped. “Howard?”

The senior man concluded his conversation before looking up at him. “Yes, Raymond?”

Ray had to drop his eyes, to search for the right words to get him started. He did not want to risk jumping straight into an argument. “We all have our orders, and we all have our priorities, I get that. It's just...Our job has always been to catch the bad guys, to lock them up, right?"

Glancing up, he saw nothing but a granite wall in the expression of the senior man. Only his eyes were dancing around, scanning Ray and trying hard to read him. "I mean, that is what we're trying to do here, catch Icarus and lock him up, right?" Ray continued. "We're not simply acting the executioner here, are we? 'Cos that never featured in our job descriptions, as I recall."

Ray's attempt to vocalise his mental wrangling ended there. He could not elaborate any further, but the older man clearly did not need to hear any more. He sighed deeply and leant forward in his chair, demanding his detectives full attention.

"Our duty is to keep law and order, and this nut job represents all that is the opposite of that," Howard explained. "The wheels are already in motion, Ray. We can only hope for both our sakes that this all works out, with this guy Lowe in a jail cell or on a morgue slab, that'll be up to him to decide." With less conviction, the older man added, "We'll do our best to bring him in and put him away, of course."

Ray did not hesitate. "Like with Trent Meadows, Chief?"

This got an instant reaction. The Chief of police visibly reddened and his chest rose and fell quicker; He was rattled. "Look, Raymond, you have to follow my lead, and I have to follow theirs," Watts jabbed a finger directly up in the air, to indicate those in office above him. "That's all you need to know. You know they want everyone to only think they are the super guys, the only people anyone could turn to for help. They have to be the ones that everyone looks up to. We can't have any Joe Schmo from the street doing a better job in two months than they done in two decades, to be the light in everyone's eye. You understand what I'm saying?"

Ray did not have to turn and look to find out, he could just sense that everyone had stopped what they were doing and were now listening in. A silence had gripped the room, and Ray could not help but feel like the admonished school boy, lectured with a guide on right and wrong that did not quite tally with his own experience. The older man had not finished, and Watts rose out of his seat to press his point home, the anger clearly bubbling beneath the surface.

"Look, okay, fuck it, lets just say for all we know, this nutcase may be just what this city needs, that he's doing a better job than we ever could, but he's still a nutcase, Knight, you know that! He belongs in a care facility, you can't argue that point with me. But if this guy don't wanna come peacefully than its up to us to do the dirty work, like we always have to. And why? Because no one else will. So, If you're not up to this, Knight, for Christ's sake out with it, because we haven't got the time or the liberty to fuck around and get all philosophical. We have an op to run, and I need to know if you're on board or not."

Ray looked up at his superior then, and whatever glimmer of hope and heaven his boss had ever possessed, could no longer be seen anywhere in those eyes. There was no refuge, no mercy there, and Ray knew he would have no say on any outcome if he was not involved. It felt like there was a collective holding of breath awaiting his response, like a sudden vacuum of oxygen in the room, and Knight forced his eyes to meet the challenge from across the desk and return the stare before he replied.

"I'm all in, Howard," Ray said in a deliberately

low and even voice. “No one wants this guy more than I do. I’ve risked everything to get on top of him, and I’m not about to let him get away.”

20

A stuttering parade of violence, of murder and atrocity, polished and presented with the appropriate commentary, to accentuate the horror and the hopelessness. Shootings, bombings, executions and armed warfare; on television, the procession was endless, and every other hour was filled with a fresh outrage or massacre, desperate to supply what the ratings demanded. Amid this swirling soup of bloodshed and carnage, a robbery, on a well known, high street bank; particularly audacious, in its use of fully automatic tactical rifles, the sum of money stolen and the fact it occurred in the mid afternoon. A cop was injured in an exchange of fire, prior to the robbers making their escape, but this was just a footnote in the reporters description.

“The police believe it to be an act of newly escaped fugitive, Trent Meadows,” Angela Draper’s face shared the screen with a police station mugshot of Meadows, his jaw held high and staring out of the photo with an angry indifference. “Ever since his brother’s death, this convicted murderer and drug importer has taken up residence in what used to be Shaun Meadows base of operations, and seemingly taken over the family business. Narcotics and crime are once again emanating from that district of the city, and Trent Meadows has made it clear, on social media and on live streams, that he is seeking vengeance on the one who killed his brother,"

This time, a grainy snippet of footage, with Trent heading a baying pack of henchmen, using two fingers to imitate a gun and pointing it into the camera lens. Snarling threats and leering gestures make it clear what he wants to do, and a chant from his companions is captured over the audio, "You're done! Son," This scene is then displaced by a frozen image of the winged man, captured by the helicopter on the night of the assault on Miles Fairmount. He is stood in shadow, his silhouette cast by the flames forming the giant dollar sign, over his shoulder.

"This has led many to question," Continued the reporter. "When and how the man of the moment, the self-styled Icarus, may respond to this challenge, and come to the rescue of the people of Templeton, as many would expect from the more traditional, silver screen superheroes most people identify with." Here, the camera zoomed back from Angela Draper, to reveal in the background her location. The steps and entrance to the city headquarters, in all its drab, concrete uniformity, hosted a small podium in front of it, currently the centre of a great deal of attention.

"The police department assure us," Draper's voice urged over the general drone of the crowd. "That tonight's conference has been called to answer this question directly, and, given their previous animosity toward Icarus, every major news broadcaster is present today to hear their take on recent events. Can they afford to continue their hunt for the city's most prominent crime fighter, who many consider a hero, or should they focus their resources on those who are truly dedicated to breaking the law and criminal activity? We here at MBS hope to hear more about this in a moment, as we go live..."

Draper is cut off, as through the headquarters main doors, Howard Watts emerged, followed closely by Tom Jameson and, a few paces behind, by Ray Knight. The Chief of police positioned himself over the central cluster of microphones and, again, rarely looking up from his notes, wasted no time in feeding the hungry crowd of reporters the information that had been so swiftly prepared and agreed upon.

"After what has happened lately and after much re-evaluation, and acknowledging the weight of public opinion, I can confirm that, in liaison with the home office, we have arrived at a different opinion on how best to handle the safety and interests of the people of this good city."

Here also, some pro-Icarus protestors had convened to make their support known; they all wore the T-shirts, many held up posters and a couple held a banner between them that read 'Icarus fights for the people, why do YOU want to stop him?' Watts noticed them only with the briefest of wary glances.

"One man cannot save the world, but, perhaps, in collaboration, like minded people can unite and work together, with a common cause, and under mutual agreement. I would like to announce this evening, that the man identified as 'Icarus', is no longer a fugitive from justice, and our mission to apprehend and detain this individual has been set aside. For my own part, if some have felt I gave too great a priority to capturing the man, then they need no longer worry, as I would like to announce my resignation from the post of Chief of Police. I will no longer be representing the head of this city's police department."

Watts waited a beat or two for this bombshell to register, before continuing. "It is our hope, and my departing wish, that we can find some way to set aside all our perceived and practical differences, and, moving forward, we would like to implore Icarus to reconsider his lone campaign of retribution, and, instead, combine forces with us, to find a common ground that we may patrol together in this city, side by side, to fight crime and bring those in breach of the law to justice."

This triggered one or two audible gasps from the journalists and silenced the protestors. Watts ploughed on. "Some may question the wisdom of joining forces with one who many might label a vigilante, or a mercenary, with a radical outlook and approach to upholding law and order. But, this is where I must draw on my own experience. I myself have stood against crime for decades in the service of the city, and have been proud to do so, and when I say I am confident that Icarus and ourselves share the same beliefs and ambitions for the place we all call home, I do not say it without some cause. Raymond?"

Watts stepped aside, and the crowd became restless, clearly not happy with letting the head of the police department off the hook so lightly, without at least a parting question or two. Ray took his place at the stand, and immediately sensed the resentment aimed his way. Already, his skin crawled with the sensation of the media's eyes turned towards him, and putting him in the spotlight. There were few places on Earth he would less like to be right then, but he forced himself forward with the notion he was nurturing, the one he had refrained from telling Watts about. The one thing that featured in this ploy he had set in motion that had some scope for partial redemption, for himself and for Icarus. The notion that somehow he may be able to brings the man in, under custody, and not under a hail of bullets.

He leant over the microphone, and heard his breathing reverberate through the powerful speakers set either side of the podium. There were so many faces, so many cameras. Ray fixed his eyes in the middle distance and concentrated on what he had had to say, and tried not to think about the millions that were potentially watching him, observing the sweat form on his brow, right at that very moment.

"I am a Detective Lieutenant of the Templeton city homicide department, and I have met with Icarus," Immediately, a wave of murmured disbelief, that Ray had to allow to recede before continuing. "He and myself have talked, in private, and I looked into the man's eyes, and he looked into mine. Unless I am very much mistaken, he is no cartoon super hero with super human powers; he is just a man, who cares about law and order, and cares about this city and its people. So, tonight, I wish to hold my hand out to this man, and ask him to join us, in a common cause to rid the streets of the gangland criminals that threaten us all. And, to facilitate this new course of action, and to demonstrate our sincerity, we wish to call upon Icarus, to call on his courage and his dedication and to meet with me, at a chosen location later tonight, to begin a new era in the protection of Templeton and its people. Meet with us, and, if we cannot rid the world of crime, at least we can try bring some safety and harmony back to the streets of our city."

In the furore that was threatening to erupt at any moment, Ray spoke louder and faster in an attempt to wind this all up quickly. “So, I will end by saying, look for the sign, Icarus. I ask you to watch the skies and look out for the symbol that will lead you to me. I will be waiting, and hoping. That is all. Thank you.”

A roar of intermingled and urgent questions followed, which neither Ray, Jameson or Watts lingered to answer, and as they hastily retreated back into headquarters, Carl Brooks could not help but laugh, as he watched it all on the big screen in interview room one.

*

He slowly closed the screen over the laptop and stared into space. Icarus played back the words in his head, sifting through them for a false step, an indicator of betrayal or dark intention. It was all so outlandish, more than even he had ever expected, like a reality suddenly coloured with fantasy.

This new life that he had constructed, this powerful, ruthless being, it was bigger and more real than he had ever imagined. Icarus was a fact, a force of nature, unstoppable, and so much so, everyone had sat up and taken notice. They had to. They had to listen, they had to react, and they had to pay attention. Everyone. There was simply no doubting his impact, his reality, his influence on the world.

It was his past life, the life in the apartment with a family and a job, that was what seemed like a dream now. A dream, that the man Lawrence Lowe had once had, in a time and place that was never truly real. A pleasant fantasy, the memory of a nice feeling, fading fast, and soon to be completely forgotten.

But still, there were doubts, and there was the matter of trust. Icarus had overcome enemies with guile and cunning, he could not afford to get sentimental and foolish now, to let ego and alter-ego cloud his sense of reason, his judgement. The reality of Icarus was in the balance, as without any resources, funds, or facilities, his operation was at an end. He was spent, burnt out. A collaboration and a new direction was attractive. He had to search among the words and determine what was likely, what was acceptable, and what he should believe in. The words offered a possible way forward, they offered the goal and the outcome he had been striving for. And they offered hope.

Here was a life line, or a deadly trap. One of the two, and he had to chose carefully which of those he would act on.

21

The missile launcher had reappeared. Someone had the notion it was an MLRS system vehicle, or something along those lines, but it did not make the hulking great vehicle any less conspicuous, and in the end, a division waved it down the road and it was backed up into an alley, out of sight and well out of harms way. In the meantime, the Templeton Police department wasted no time in getting set up and prepared for engagement.

There was an uneasy balance to be struck; enough officers and back up had to be on hand, but at the same time, they did not want to crowd the immediate area. For one, it was thought it might alert Icarus and deter him from showing, and two, a giant gathering of police officers was likely to alert the roaming news networks and attract great crowds of unwanted spectators. Watts and tactics made the call, and half the task force was accompanied by two response units and a half dozen strategically located patrol cars, the departments fastest.

Mercifully, the rain had eased off that evening, but the temperature had dropped into low single figures. Most of the men were pleased to be wearing their body armour and Watts and the task force were well wrapped up. Right then, Williams was unloading some heavy duty storage boxes full of long, black, deadly looking things, distributing them to a half dozen of his men, and deploying them in pairs onto the upper floors of the three major high rises around them. The main building they had selected for the hopeful rendez-vous was the Templeton natural history museum and arts gallery, which, with its Art Deco pinnacle and viewing platform, was considered to be tall enough, prominent enough, and suitably neutral to all concerned. It was also known to be closed and emptied for the evening, so they could reasonably expect minimum disturbance and interference.

Everyone could not resist speaking in hushed tones, as if that would aid their mission of secrecy. Even Watts was unusually tactful and cautious in his directions, using the full range of body language and gestures to get his messages across, He was fizzing with nerves and jumpy with it, of course, as was everyone else. Everyone except Williams, that is, who was like a kid at Christmas with all the toys he suddenly had at his disposal. Lalonde was still on medical leave for the first degree burns sustained during the last ambush, so his tactical number two was now running the show. As he was issuing the sniper team with their semi automatic rifles, Watts was clucking and fussing over their shoulders like an over protective mother, reminding and chastening them to choose their shots carefully and promise to do their best not to damage the masonry of one of the city's most revered buildings.

"Mid torso targets only, roger that, Chief."

A helicopter flew over head. "Is that one ours?" Watts asked Jameson, behind him, who came off the radio to confirm that it was and would be ready in position in five minutes. Everything seemed to be taking shape nicely, and the sense of anticipation in the air was electric.

Knight was not excited, however. He was sickened by the sight of arms and deadly force being deployed all around him, and with an ever increasing, hollowed out feeling of dread and doom, he surveyed the manoeuvres and marching-to-orders occurring all about him. There was nothing comic, courageous or even remotely honourable going on here, Ray observed. With an increasingly pained grimace etched on his features, he stood on the side walk and wondered at it all. It looked like they were preparing for the arrival of Godzilla.

As an ominous roll of thunder rumbled from the skies above, the last of the storage boxes was unpacked, and a giant spot light with supporting fixtures was lifted out from its foam bedding. Watts hurried over to inspect the thin steel stencil that was tacked over the face of the lens, and after a moment of humming and harrumphing, he nodded and swept his hand up to send the men away and into the museum with it. Before he could get distracted again, Ray sidled up to his ex boss and cleared his throat.

"Chief, perhaps I should go up with the beacon? I want to be there when they light it up, in case our man is itching to meet with me."

Watts regarded the detective severely from down his chin. "What's with all this 'I' and meet 'me' shit? I was thinking Jameson and Williams would do the meet?"

"Why would he trust them?" Ray risked raising his voice, making his indignation and protest clear. "Listen, we can't afford to take any risks with him backing out. We got a much better chance if there is just one of us there, and someone he recognises. He knows me already."

"He didn't exactly roll out the red carpet for you as I recall, Knight. You sure he hasn't got a grudge to bear for your role in the Darlow plea?"

Ray swallowed. "We talked through that."

This was a stand-off, but Ray refused to back down. He tried being reasonable. "I know the risks, Chief, but you heard me at the conference. I made a promise to the man."

Another long moment of silence, but then Watts blinked first. "Peters! Williams!" he yelled, and the profile and evaluation man joined the other two in an intense huddle, that Ray could only watch from the outside. This is it, he thought. Do or die time.

There was an exchange of shrugs, and then eventually Watts turned back round to face him. If he was impressed at all with Ray's valour and commitment, he hid it well. "Okay, Knight. It's your show. But you can be sure we'll all be watching very closely, you follow me?"

Before Ray could ask what he meant by that, everyone stopped what they were doing and to a man, their necks hinged over as they all looked up into the sky. High above them, from the very peak of the building, the signal had been cast, and the image of the winged man was beamed out into the night and over the top of the city.

22

Sixteen storeys high, the wind billowed overhead in shifting clouds of muted blues and shadowy black masses. Occasional gusts carried with them icy raindrops, which peppered the surfaces of concrete and steel on the rooftop and made everything slippery. Beneath, and all around, Templeton city glowed like an artificial constellation, blinking and twinkling to the horizon, as distant and alien to Ray right then as any remote galaxy could be.

And constantly above him, the thick beacon of light, penetrating the darkness with the message at the end of its beam. The winged man, summoned and lured to this place, at the behest of the people, and of the police. Come, fight crime with us, we need you. *We need you to come, so we can gun you down like a rabid animal!*

Ray shivered and squeezed his jacket closer around him, pulling the lapels up to his jaw, but he could not keep out the cold any more than he could the feeling of unrelenting anxiousness. Along with the countless eyes fixed on this exact spot, impatiently wanting to see what would happen next, there was a multitude of gun barrels and scope sights aimed right at this location as well.

Did he really believe there could be any other outcome, other than him leading Icarus to sacrifice? Rays thoughts were divided by the wretchedness he would feel for serving up the winged avenger, and the absurdity of his intention to do otherwise.

If he could somehow appeal to the man behind the monster, the reasonable man lost in the lunacy, then maybe they could both leave this building alive. A negotiated surrender, in the seconds between meeting and one of the many snipers pulling just too tightly on their trigger. Just a little more pressure, and he felt he would snap; crumble to the ground, curl up and let wretchedness take him.

Ray forced his breath out so he could force a fresh lungful in, and recapture some regular pattern to his heartbeat and some control over his nerves. All thoughts of smoking for once were entirely absent; he needed something far stronger than nicotine to restore calm, and also he knew that the cigarette in his fingers would expose the trembling he felt in his limbs. He had to grip himself closely, knit and tense all his muscles at once, to try and maintain the strength and courage for what he had to try and do.

How long had he been up here already? An hour, an hour and a half? The news networks would be gathering soon, more sets of eyes, watching his every move, every thought cross his face. He went back to pacing, slowly, from the end of the roof top where the viewing platform began to the restaurant end with the doorway to the stair well. What if the man did not show up? This whole enterprise would be a waste of time, he would be humiliated and disgraced, and the vigilante would go on, likely to be shot down or drone-striked on a later mission. Ray wondered if that could be a preferable outcome, one where he was not responsible for the super hero's demise. Maybe, just maybe, Lawrence Lowe could get shot and incapacitated to the extent where he could be taken in, and not just ruthlessly dispatched under gunfire. It was possible, not likely, but possible, despite what he knew about the gun squads reluctance to take any chances.

If there was a genuine alternative, a solution that he could convince himself of, then it was too late anyway. He had to stay and wait and hope that Icarus came. *I hope he doesn't fucking come!*

In the all-green haze of night vision, the dark figure of Raymond Knight moved from left to right and back again along an eighty foot span, which was tracked in the scope mounted on sniper five's rifle. He was stationed on the top of the Liberty Bank building just to the East of the museum, lying prone behind a raised brick parapet, and the sniper shifted his head slightly to alleviate a crick developing in his neck. It was then the figure in the scope sights halted abruptly.

A sound, possibly of a pigeon taking off or landing. Ray moved to look at the eaves of the roof top, squinting against the intermittent drizzle, following the line of the facia rising to thick electric cables branching off of the enormous antenna at the peak of the building. He let his focus trail upward into the blackness beyond, almost expecting the winged figure to descend from the heavens like the super human the media wanted to portray him as. An Impossible fantasy designed to distract and rejuvenate the masses from their largely dull, gruelling lives.

The reality was here, in the cold and alone, under the sight of a gun barrel, with orders of shoot to kill. Ray had had enough. He let the next gust of wind turn him around and marched toward the fire exit. Lawrence Lowe was not coming, he was too smart for that, and they were just wasting their time, and the tax payers money.

He swung open the door and started down the stairs, and at the next landing, drew up straight in shock as a tall dark figure, trailing a long, black cape, swept up from the floor below. Icarus stopped too, and the pair of them regarded each other in silence for a second. It was no "superhero" that Ray looked upon then, more like a cheap, cosplay outfit from a toy store. He could not identify any armour or weaponry at all, but the icy blue eyes were as fierce as ever

"Lawrence, listen to me," Ray began, but the other man interrupted him.

"I told you not to call me that. You have lied to me," he raised a hand to point an accusing finger at the detective, his voice thick with anger and emotion.. "Every word you said was a lie. The block is crawling with police and I saw two armed officers follow in behind me. They're on their way up here now. This was all just a trap!"

Ray had to keep his voice under control if he had any hope of trying to convince the person who was advancing upon him now with aggressive purpose. "I know, it is a trap Icarus. They want you dead, of course they do! What did you expect? That is why you must come with me. Let me take you in, Icarus, and together we can walk out of here. Its the only way."

"Bullshit! Another trap, more lies..." He was a couple of steps from him now and looming large. Ray tried raising his voice, to match the anger in the others tone.

"It is not! I owe you for what I did. You were right, I did not get justice for you and your family, I admit it. But you have to believe me that the only way you're going to get out of this building alive is in my custody. Let me help you..."

"Help? By offering me up to the mercy of the corrupt court officials, for judgement by the very same people who protect the pillaging, greedy corporations?"

They came face to face, Ray a good head shorter, so he had to look up into those fearsome eyes. He tried to hold his gaze steady and make his voice sound reasonable.

"Better that then dead. Think of the coverage of the court case, the opportunity you will have to be heard. Everyone will be watching." And on a lower octave. "And think of your other child, Lawrence. Is it fair to her, to leave her behind?"

He saw the man tense, his hands bunch into a fist, and he wondered if he had pushed it too far, but it was then that they both heard the noise. Footfall, racing up steps. As one, they ducked over the railing to look below, and saw the black, armoured figures forging toward them, making a spiral of bodies snaking upward

"I must leave." Icarus turned for the roof.

"Wait, you step out that door and a dozen spot lights will come on and a dozen more snipers will open fire. You'll never make it."

The winged man shook off the detectives grip on his forearm. "I have a chute, under the cape. If I can get over the side of the roof, I can deploy..."

Ray shook his head. "Impossible! There's

choppers and ground teams. they'll surround you before you reach the ground. You have to come with me, its your only chance!" His voice became an imploring yell at the end, but the winged vigilante stood firm and rigid, like a blank brick wall.

"The odds are always stacked against us, Detective. That's the system we must fight against. I am ready to be a martyr to the cause. Are you?"

"Wait," was all Ray could think to say. "Just give me a second."

*

The instruction had gone out over the radio, in shortened code. Everyone was on full alert and prepared to fire, and none more so than sniper five. He was motionless, his arms and his rifle as one, and the image in the scope all he could see. The museum rooftop had been empty ever since that officer had left, but now the fire escape door swung open once more. He shifted the sight to cover the portal, and tightened his finger over the trigger as he observed a figure emerge from the stairwell. A heartbeat, and he recognised the detective from before, allowing his grip on the trigger to relax just slightly. His sights kept the man in dead centre, as he turned to move across to the other side of the roof.

"Hold your fire," a voice came over the crackle of the radio, before it went dead again. "Identify the target."

His sights zipped from the empty doorway and back to the police officer. The adrenalin was rising and with it came confusion, as he observed the detective begin to mount the rig attached to side of the viewing platform. In the next instant, his retina were scorched by a sudden blaze of blinding whiteness.

It took all of Ray's strength to grip the wide lens and twist the rig on its pivot, pulling the mechanism around and making the signal beam swoop down and over the adjacent rooftops. He directed the powerful shaft of light as well as he could judge toward the waiting eyes of the snipers, slowly pivoting the mechanism around to dazzle as many as he could. He felt like the soldier in a gun turret, swinging the heavy cannon around toward the enemy

With that thought, came the first bullet. He heard a quiet fizz and then a loud clang as the metal bracket at his feet erupted into sparks. This was closely followed by a further three or four rounds, one zipping over Rays head with a discernible whining sound, while another clanged into the metal of the railing beside him. His shoulders screaming with control of the spotlight and his back in spasms trying to hunch behind the rig at the same time for cover, Ray was certain one of the bullets was about to ricochet into his torso, and that was when all hell broke loose.

A roaring torrent of bullets suddenly rained across in a barrage of gunfire as Icarus made his dash for the edge of the building. Several bullets collided into the lens and abruptly ended the light beam, one of them travelling through the rig and exiting beside Rays ear. The glass shattered outward and an angry arc of electricity jolted the mechanism out of Ray's hands and sent him tumbling over into the path of the lethal ballistic cascade.

From the corner of his eye, Ray glimpsed a human form, silhouetted against the myriad lights of the city's skyscrapers, leap up and over the far side of the railing, while rifle rounds embedded into the walls and sparked off the steel strutting all around him. A second later, and the chaos of gun fire receded, as the target dropped out of sight

Ray forced himself to his feet, and in some state of shock, staggered over to the side of the building. If he had taken a hit, he could not feel anything, and was only aware of an overriding compulsion to discover where the winged man had gone. Grasping onto the slick and slippery railing circling the expanse of the buildings peak, he craned his head over the side and searched feverishly for any sight of the super hero.

Amid the kaleidoscope of swimming blinks and flashes beneath him, Ray picked out a rectangle of canvas suddenly blossom into being about half way down the buildings side; Icarus's parachute. Squinting to maintain focus, Ray's eyes tracked the form swing out over the streets and swoop across the distance between this building and the next. As Icarus approached the glass edifice opposite, a motion came from above and there came over the wind an odd roar and wooshing sound. A projectile passed within feet of the looping parachutist and then disappeared into the building beside him. In the next second, an explosion engulfed the image of the canvas rectangle, and that side of the far building was awash with smoke as a ball of flame travelled up its side only to disperse as it reached the upper floors.

Ray could feel some of the heat from that explosion, and also some of the shock wave. As he watched, the parachute emerged from the cloud of smoke, the canvas now in flames, and the trajectory sent in a spinning, erratic confusion. The desent was no longer gradual, and the burning remnants of Icarus's brief flight plummeted out of focus and down to the streets below. Ray sank to his knees, and closed his eyes. He did not want to see any more.

23

The images in the next morning's news were mirrored across all the channels. The grey, drizzly late-autumn weather obscured any magnified details, but the police officers and ambulance crew were clearly defined, busily clustered around the banks of the great river. There was some speculation - or hope, perhaps - that Icarus may have survived the fiery descent from the skies as it ended in the filthy brown waters of the Dunster, similar to his escape from the Fairmount building. Morbid glimpses of a stretcher bearing a body-shaped form quickly quashed that idea, however.

"Police sources confirm that the body recovered from the river earlier this morning was in fact that of Lawrence Lowe, better known to the people of Templeton as 'Icarus'," Angela Draper appeared genuinely sombre, even around her usually vivid blue eyes, as she spoke to camera. Perhaps in reverence for the end of one of the richest periods of news ratings the channel had seen for a long time.

Lieutenant Fletcher snapped off the television, on an order barked from behind him. Interview room one was being returned to its original purpose, and the ex Chief of police was expecting a busy afternoon of conferences with various politicos and bigwigs, all needing reassurances that their careers were safe and to get all their stories straight. Howard Watts would have liked to have some assurance on his own career, but the stink from the manner of how Icarus was despatched was yet to be fully absorbed. Fortunately, there was word of fresh atrocities and blood-shed from the Trent Meadows cartel, so media attention would likely be diverted that way, everyone hoped.

In all, it was very much like a normal, if greatly subdued afternoon at police headquarters, and little attention was paid to Raymond Knights' return from debriefing. He had mumbled and blanked out much of that encounter, until the familiar female counsellor from staff welfare had intervened. There had been no quips or bravado this time; Ray was more than glad to see her, and gratefully accepted her charity, along with the potent anti-anxiety medication and two days leave.

In a groggy fug of mixed emotions and weariness, Ray ambled in the direction of his desk, ignoring the hails of concern and surprised expressions of his colleagues. Although his participation in the case was effectively ended, there was still the unpleasant aftermath to be handled, and for Ray at least, a queasy and oppressive question mark hanging over everything. *Vague*, thought Knight, already considering the report he may have to write up.

Lost in his thoughts, the detective almost bumped into Howard Watts coming out of his office. The older man studied him up and down warily.

"Still here, Knight?"

Ray regarded his ex boss with blank apathy, compounded by the nullifying effects of the medication. The question mark hovering over the case and within his befuddled mind seemed to focus into something like clarity right then, and Ray managed to croak out a response.

"You know, Chief, maybe, if we'd just let Lowe get away from us, like so many other crooks, we'd all be sitting in a better world right now, you ever think of that?"

Watts' face remained a grim mask of disapproval, until, in the end, his eyes softened and he opted to give just the slightest of shrugs.

"I'm being forced into early retirement, Raymond," The older man said. "I guess I'll have plenty of time to think about that, along with a million other things. Shit, you know how it is."

Ray could think of no response to that, so he turned around and made to leave the building. "Yeah," he said over his shoulder. "I know how it is."

*

The city was as ever cold, grim and imposing, but it was still very busy. Traffic roared and the people swelled and flowed. It was almost as if everyone else in Templeton that day could not bare to watch the story unfold on the news, and had forced themselves out, onto the streets, instead. Anything seemed preferable that day, and inconsequential tasks and errands were now urgent.

Ray strolled along the pavement, in no hurry, as he usually was when he traversed the distance between his work place and his apartment. He was in no rush to return to that place, not even with the clear threat of rain. The relentless weather and the noisy chaos he could shut out. His thoughts, he was stuck with.

It was difficult to make any sense of them. To dwell on memory was a luxury few could afford, and the relentless grind of life and the hyper diversion of the media all too quickly caused significant moments to fade. Recollections and images, like the skies filled with searchlights and bullets fizzing through the air, they would all eventually get washed away by the constant fall of rain and the passage of time. Even the bright, innocent shine of a child's smile could become distant and irretrievable, forever lost in some other life.

It was a far brighter thought he had then that could not be dampened by any downpour. He had decided he was going to head to his wife's place, and stop by there for a while. His ex wife. And, maybe, if he was lucky, he would see his daughter there, as well. He hoped so, and he hoped too that they may talk, and catch up with each other's lives.

Ray paused by a digital appliance store, and glanced in at the big television screen there. He blinked, and then leant a little closer. A man in a dark suit and cape, very familiar-looking, was depicted scrambling across a street and out of shot down an alleyway. Beneath the footage, a banner headline read in big white text;

'Copycat hero foils street mugging'

The effects of the medication and his all round exhaustion made it hard for Ray to decide how to react to this. He just stared at the television screen, while in the streets behind him, the rain began to fall.

If you enjoyed this book, find out more about the sequel now ...

the Knight Terrors

See over for sneak preview

For the first 20 ordered, HALF PRICE read & reviewed on Amazon !

email the publisher or contact Raymond Knight on Facebook for info on how to grab up these offers or get a Personalised Signed Copy

A series of unusual deaths

An unholy gang of street kids

and a cop about to become ...
... afraid of the dark !

Detective Raymond Knight is about to be drawn into another case that that will challenge all that he sees, and all that he believes possible

A suspect is in custody - barely ten years old - and the bloody trail leads back to a condemned apartment block haunted by tragic events, and the remnants of a crew of youths intent on raising hell...

Can Ray Knight unravel the mystery before he succombs to

the Knight Terrors

email today to see the trailer for the new book , or watch it on YouTube or at Raymond Knights facebook page.

about the Author

A paranormal investigator and videographer most of the time, when he's not marking exams for Cambridge University, Alex Cousins will be found scribbling some new masterpiece or attempting to launch the production of a horror movie from one of his scripts. Currently, he is finishing a series of illustrated young readers fiction, scheduled for publication sometime in the new year.

Printed in Great Britain
by Amazon